OTHER YEARLING BOOKS YOU WILL ENJOY:

THE SYLVIA GAME, *Vivien Alcock*
THE MONSTER GARDEN, *Vivien Alcock*
THE MYSTERIOUS MR. ROSS, *Vivien Alcock*
TRAVELERS BY NIGHT, *Vivien Alcock*
THE HAUNTING OF CASSIE PALMER, *Vivien Alcock*
DEVIL-IN-THE-FOG, *Leon Garfield*
FOOTSTEPS, *Leon Garfield*
THE NIGHT OF THE COMET, *Leon Garfield*
THE MOFFATS, *Eleanor Estes*
THE MIDDLE MOFFAT, *Eleanor Estes*

YEARLING BOOKS/YOUNG YEARLINGS/YEARLING CLASSICS are designed especially to entertain and enlighten young people. Patricia Reilly Giff, consultant to this series, received the bachelor's degree from Marymount College. She holds the master's degree in history from St. John's University, and a Professional Diploma in Reading from Hofstra University. She was a teacher and reading consultant for many years, and is the author of numerous books for young readers.

For a complete listing of all Yearling titles,
write to Dell Readers Service,
P.O. Box 1045, South Holland, IL 60473.

The Stonewalkers

Vivien Alcock
AR B.L.: 4.7
Points: 4.0

UG

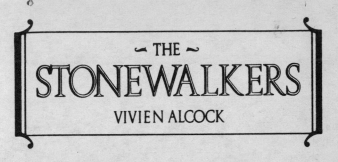

~ THE ~
# STONEWALKERS
VIVIEN ALCOCK

A Yearling Book

Published by
Dell Publishing
a division of
Bantam Doubleday Dell Publishing Group, Inc.
666 Fifth Avenue
New York, New York 10103

This work was first published in Great Britain by Methuen Children's
Books Ltd.
Copyright © 1981 by Vivien Alcock

ISBN: 0-440-40300-6

Reprinted by arrangement with Delacorte Press

Printed in the United States of America

June 1990

10 9 8 7 6 5 4 3 2 1

OPM

To Sylvia and Colin

1

It was a summer of sudden thunder. The first storm came one Wednesday in July. Hot! It was the sort of day when the earth cracks, dogs run mad, and even friends are best avoided. The sky, which only half an hour ago had been a dry blue, now thickened with dark clouds. Soon it was going to rain very hard, and anyone caught far from shelter would be soaked to the skin.

The girl sitting in the long grass at the foot of the statue did not seem to notice. Her name was Poppy Brown, and she was a liar. It was the only remarkable thing about her. She was twelve years old, neither tall nor short, dark nor fair, fat nor thin, pretty nor plain. An ordinary child except for her lies.

These stood out in a crowd for being so much taller than anyone else's. Her mother was a trapeze artist, she'd claim, who'd fallen in a flash of spangles, missed the safety net, and was now in the hospital with broken bones. Her father was a great hunter, away catching elephants for an Indian prince; she was going to join him during the holidays. These lies came from her lips like pretty soap bubbles, doomed to shatter helplessly on the first hard corner of fact. (Her mother was a cook and her father had died when she was three years old.)

"Why?" she'd be asked. "Why, Poppy? You must've known we'd find out—" and she'd shake her head, her blue eyes filling with tears, as sorrowful and puzzled as anyone.

There was a time when she'd tried to be helpful, not liking to see them so at a loss. "Mrs. Martin says I've got too much imagination," she'd offer, or "Mrs. Welsh says it's because I've been shopped around so much." She soon learned to keep quiet. They didn't like a child to be too knowing and would say sharply that there were plenty of children far worse off than she was who managed to tell the truth. She was one of the lucky ones. She had a mother to love her and make a home for her whenever possible. It was not her mother's fault that this was not possible more often. Mrs. Brown was not strong. . . .

When Poppy was five, her mother had gone into the hospital for so long that when at last Poppy was allowed to see her, she did not recognize her and would have walked past the pale, gaunt woman in the bed, had not Foster-Mother Allen caught hold of her arm and told her to go and kiss her mother. She had sat uncomfortably on the chair, while her mother gazed at her pleadingly, as if she wanted something. But Poppy had already given her the flowers.

And when she had started to tell her mother about the school play, Mrs. Brown had not seemed interested and had, in fact, fallen asleep, so Poppy had been led away.

Since then her mother had been in and out of the hospital so often that Poppy lost count. Mrs. Brown had had to give up her job in the café in Camden Town, taking instead, when she was well enough, live-in jobs where she was not always able to have Poppy. She refused to go on welfare. Something seemed to drive her to work, as if she were trying to make up for all those long weeks lying in bed doing nothing. She was not content just to look after Poppy.

"She wants to make a good home for you, dear," they told her. "You know that she loves you."

"Oh, yes!"

Yes, her mother loved her; she was a child of many mothers, real, house, and foster, and they all loved her. She knew this because they told her so. She was grateful—she knew better than to look a gift horse in the mouth, especially when it kept showing its teeth. But she had no high opinion of love. Love did not stop people from being angry with you and punishing you for your own good. Love was not blind to your faults, but sought them out—to grieve over. Love did not delight in your company but openly showed its relief when it was time for you to go—back to school or to bed or merely the other side of the door. "Run along and play, dearie." Not *stay* and play, oh, no! Remove yourself and be quick about it!

"I'd much rather just be *liked*," she told the statue. She often talked to the statue. It was a good listener. She told it everything—her hopes, her fears, confessions even, knowing it was quite safe. The statue would never tell. And at the moment she had no other friends.

It was very quiet in this forgotten part of the garden. Very still. The birds had all flown away to their trees, where they sat close together, wrapped in their wings. The small white butterflies no longer hung about the old lavender like agitated blossom. The sky grew darker. But the girl in the red dress, Poppy in the long grass, did not look up. Her head drooped over her hands, so that her soft, mouse-colored hair almost obscured her face. She was pulling the seeds off a head of grass, one by one—yes . . . no . . . yes . . . no . . . yes. Whatever answer the grass gave her did not seem to please her, for she flung the stalk away crossly.

"Never meet trouble halfway," she advised the statue. "It may be going next door. Never cross your bridges before they're built. Besides, I may be run over by a bus tomorrow. Why spoil my last day?"

The statue remained silent and smiling, its pale eyes, hollow in the center, fixed in their carved lids to gaze endlessly at the sky. It looked very beautiful in the stormy light.

"Did you ever hear of the lady of Devizes?" Poppy asked, fiddling now with her bracelet. "One of my mothers took me to Devizes once."

She had been quite small, but she still remembered it. A pretty little country town with a marketplace. It wasn't market day, and she'd been disappointed, having heard there would be calves and sheep in pens, and stalls of jumble and jewelry, fruit and flowers. Instead she had been taken by the hand across the bare cobbles and shown the monument in the middle of the square. In memory of a woman, long ago, who on being accused of giving short measure had cried aloud in ringing tones, "May God strike me dead if I tell a lie!" He did. The townspeople had erected the monument to commemorate the event.

"See what I mean? Silly thing to say, wasn't it? God might not've gotten around to it for years if she'd kept her big mouth shut."

The sky grew darker. Leaves shuddered suddenly on the bushes and were still again. Insects hurried through the grass seeking shelter. An ant ran over Poppy's leg and she put out her hand to brush it off. Her bracelet slipped over her fingers and fell to the ground. It was too big. She picked it up and swung it idly to and fro.

"Isn't it pretty?" she asked the statue. "I made it myself." She noticed it had left a dirty mark on her wrist where she'd been sweating. And it was too big. "You have it, Belladonna," she said generously, and fastened it around one of the statue's ankles. It was made of an odd, greenish-black metal, part of some old chain she'd found in the cellar.

"Now you look like a slave, waiting to be set free."

The statue smiled, its calm and beautiful face white against the black sky—black sky at four in the afternoon! Poppy jumped to her feet as the first drop fell. She was halfway across the overgrown lawn when the forked tongue of lightning sprang down from the clouds and licked toward her. . . .

Flat on the ground, her face buried in the grass, thunder crashed about her ears and the sky fell.

She was not dead. She was not burned to a cinder. The rain falling heavily on her back did not sizzle. Cautiously she opened her eyes and raised her head. At the same moment the statue, fallen from its pedestal onto the grass a few yards away, raised its head also, and they stared at one another, both so white and motionless that it was difficult to tell which girl was made of stone.

2

They'll never believe *this*! was the first thought that came into her head, as clear and plain as if written on white paper. Come to that, she didn't believe it herself. Poppy, dear girl, she told herself, shutting her eyes tight and beginning to tremble, you may be the biggest liar out of hell, but you're not so far around the bend that you can't see both ways. Belladonna's made of stone, and stones can't raise their heads and look where they please. You're dreaming, that's what it is, and the rain thumping on your back is because you left your window open; and the grass tickling your nose is a feather popped out of your pillow. Open your eyes and you'll find yourself tucked snug in bed.

But she kept her eyes squeezed shut, for one thought follows another, and her bed wasn't under the window nor had her pillow a feather to fly with, being made of foam rubber and smooth as a rubber boot.

Try again, Poppy. The lightning struck the

bracelet, the stone cracked, the statue fell. Its head broke off and bounced up off the grass to look at you. Open your eyes and you'll see she's not lying propped up on her elbow staring at you but scattered all around in bits and pieces.

Her eyelids flared scarlet and there was another crash of thunder. The rain seemed to be trying to push her into the ground. No good staying there to be drowned. She opened her eyes. True enough, the statue was no longer lying propped up on its elbow staring at her. It was now sitting bolt upright on the grass staring at her.

"Oh, Lord above!" whispered Poppy.

The stone mouth opened and cracks ran from it like spiders over the pale cheeks.

"Your face . . ." whispered Poppy, but even as she spoke, the rain pouring over the marble cheeks seemed to wash the cracks away, leaving them as white and smooth as before. Then the statue made a low, groaning noise, quite horrible to hear, like a record put on at the wrong speed, as if it were trying to speak but hadn't quite got the hang of it.

"Go away!" cried Poppy.

She herself could not move. It was not so much that she was rooted to the ground as slowly sinking into it. Her legs and belly were made of mud by the feel of them, and useless for running.

Very slowly the statue got to its feet, moving its limbs with effort as if through deep water, and cracks running everywhere before they were smoothed out by the rain. It groaned again and began coming toward her, rocking slightly on stiff legs and sinking into the wet grass at every step.

Poppy pushed herself up onto her trembling legs. No good trying to hide in the mud like a worm. Face the facts, she told herself, face the facts: Lightning struck statue, statue came to life. It's a mutation, that's what it is.

The word comforted her as she stood gaping; it sounded scientific. Men had once been apes, after all, and then for no reason she'd ever been told, suddenly they put clothes on and decided to be men. So a statue had come to life—why not? Why be frightened? Anyway, she could outrun it any time she chose, and would do so, too, if it came one step nearer.

The statue stopped and stood where it was, just out of arm's reach, the long grass up to its knees.

Lightning flickered behind its head some way off, and the thunder lagged behind. Rain, which had been falling straight down as if guided by a ruler, now came sideways in untidy gusts, parting Poppy's hair at the back and blowing right into the statue's face. It gazed at her with its wet eyes and then . . . began to smile. The cracks came finer now, like those on an old plate, and were soon washed away. It smiled and very slowly began to move its right arm, forward and up—as if it wanted to shake hands!

Why, I do believe it's friendly, Poppy thought,

amazed. Yet, why not? Who'd sat and talked to it for many an hour when it stood lonely on its pedestal? Befriended it and given it a pretty name? (Poppy knew Belladonna was a flower. She did not know it was another name for deadly nightshade, against which she had been warned, for its berries are poisonous and can kill.) Who'd given it the bracelet, the chain that had helped to bring it to life?

Why, it probably thinks you're God, Poppy Brown! Or its mother! How will it feel if you turn your back on it now and run off? Sick, cold, deserted, that's how it will feel, with a sort of pain somewhere inside that will never quite go away. It's all alone, too, the only one of its kind in the whole world.

Poppy whispered, "You poor old thing," and smiled back at it. They stood smiling at each other while the rain blew about them.

"Well, it's no good standing here catching our deaths," Poppy said at last. "You'd better come along with me, my pretty. Though Lord knows what they'll make of you up at the house!"

Beckoning to it and looking often over her shoulder, she led the way from the little wilderness with the empty pedestal, through the dripping shrubbery, and across the smooth lawns to the house. The statue, smiling and moaning, lumbered after her. Its feet cut deep holes in the old, pampered turf, which, filling rapidly with water, shone like little ponds to mark the way they'd come. When it reached the edge of the lawn, it stopped.

Poppy, waiting on the flagged path, thought perhaps it was nervous, never having seen a house so close before, and said encouragingly, "Come on, my own"—although of course it was not her own at all but belonged to Mr. Hunt, like the house and the grounds and the very bed Poppy slept in. It occurred to Poppy for the first time to wonder if her mother's employer would be pleased to have one of his statues come to life. He was not supposed to be overfond of company. Still, no good crying over spilled milk. What's done was done.

"No one's going to believe in you," she said. "Still, seeing's believing, I suppose, as the prisoner said to blind Justice. Come on!"

Obediently the statue walked forward onto the path.

Bang! Bang! Bang!

The marble feet crashed against the paving stones with a noise far sharper than thunder.

"Stop!" Poppy cried in dismay, holding her hand up to halt it. "You'll bring Mr. Hunt down on us. I'm not supposed to make noise near the house. Couldn't you sort of slide your feet along like this . . . ?"

Scrape! Scrape! Scrape!

It was worse, if anything. And how muddy her feet were!

They reached a door in the side of the house, which Poppy opened.

"Here we are," she said, beckoning the statue forward. "There's a sink in here. We can make ourselves all spick and span before I take you to see Mother Brown. Mrs. Brown, my real mother, that is. She doesn't like dirt. Mud on your feet and she wouldn't notice if you wore a halo. Sit on that chair while I run the water."

It was a wooden chair and it stood no chance. The heavy statue crashed right through it with a tremendous clattering bang onto the floor. Three flowerpots fell off a shelf and broke, scattering their earth. The statue's smile now looked like a grimace of pain. Or anger.

"Oh! Oh, I'm sorry, I didn't think. . . ." Poppy rushed to its side. "You're not broken, are you? Chipped? Let me help you up!"

Its arm felt cold, like marble—and yet not *quite* like marble anymore. But nothing, no, nothing like flesh and blood. Though she tugged with both hands, Poppy should not shift it, and it seemed to make no effort to help itself.

"Oh, you're hurt! I'll fetch Mother Brown! She'll know what to do. I won't be long!"

The statue, left alone, slowly turned its head to look around the room. Its gaze became fixed. On the shelf there was the marble head of a girl, on a black base. It stared at this for some time, and its hand moved stiffly to touch its own neck. When it looked back toward the door, the friendly innocence of its face was quite gone. It wore an expression of cold mistrust.

3

In the kitchen the two women heard the crash. Too loud for thunder! Wrong sort of noise! Mrs. Robbins turned from the sink and stared at Mrs. Brown. Mrs. Brown, her hands poised over a bowl of flour, stared back. Then, hearing footsteps thudding down the passage toward them, they both turned to stare at the door. It burst open.

Poppy, leaning in the doorway, trying to recover her breath, thought how funny they looked, like dummies, each holding up her hands as if in amazement; one pair in pink rubber gloves and the other white with flour. Mrs. Robbins's face relaxed when she saw who it was, as if she had expected a monster at least, but Mrs. Brown looked as though she thought her daughter quite bad enough.

"What have you done now?" she asked in a voice as sharp as her elbows.

"Noth—nothing! It's—"

"What was that 'orrible noise?" asked Mrs. Robbins, "Aven't 'urt yourself, 'ave you, love?"

"No. It's—"

"You're all wet," said Mrs. Robbins, coming up and inspecting Poppy with round brown eyes, "But it ain't blood. 'Oo's 'urt then?" she asked hopefully. "Mr. 'Unt fallen downstairs and broke 'is neck, 'as 'e?"

Mrs. Robbins was a Londoner. After ten years in Charle, she still found country life a bit slow. She missed the bustle and excitement of London, with police cars and ambulances screaming through the night, while she was safe in bed. Not, of course, that she wished anybody any real harm!

But Poppy shook her head.

"It's Belladonna," she said. The women looked blank. "The *statue*—the one from the little garden. It's fallen down! I can't lift it—it's so heavy! Please come! I think it's hurt."

"If you've broken something that costs a lot—" said her mother, her face nearly as white as the flour on her hands. "A statue—oh, Lord! I told you to be careful! I *told* you! If you've cost me my job, I—I don't know what—"

She broke off as Mrs. Robbins laid a pink, rubber-gloved hand on her arm.

"There, there, dearie! Don't take on. 'E won't turn you out. 'Ow did it 'appen?" she asked, turning to Poppy.

"It wasn't me!" said Poppy, looking uneasily at her mother. "It was the lightning. I'm not responsible for lightning, am I? I'm not Jove or whoever it is up there! The lightning struck the statue—and then—"

She couldn't say it. It was true but it wasn't going to sound that way. She could've told Mrs. Robbins, but not with her mother standing there with that long-suffering look. . . .

"Oh, lightning, was it?" Mrs. Robbins said comfortably. "Act of God. Nothing to do with us. Out in the garden, you said. Not our job to clear it away, then. Mr. Shepherd, 'e's in charge of the garden. Your ma and me, we're only the 'ouse."

"It's *in* the house now! Please come!" Poppy exclaimed urgently, seeing Mrs. Robbins settle herself comfortably on a chair and begin to peel off her gloves, as if she'd lost all interest. "It's in that little room with the sink where we leave our boots—"

"'Ow did it get there, then?" asked Mrs. Robbins, interested.

"IT WALKED!" shouted Poppy, furious that the truth should sound so much less probable than even the wildest of her lies. Everything was going wrong. As usual. "Don't believe me! I'm not asking you to believe me!" she cried, seeing her mother's face. "Just come and see for yourselves—that's all!"

"I've a good mind to wash your mouth out with soap," her mother said angrily.

"It's not the only thing that needs washing," said Mrs. Robbins, winking at Poppy behind her mother's back. "Better get 'er out of them wet

{ 17 }

clothes and into an 'ot bath before you spank 'er, Mrs. Brown, or we'll 'ave an invalid on our 'ands."

"Please come, Mother Brown," pleaded Poppy, taking hold of her mother's arm. It felt as hard as the statue's, only warmer and rougher.

"Don't call me Mother Brown," her mother muttered under her breath. "Just Mother is enough. Or Mom."

But Poppy was out of the kitchen. She could hear the two women following her down the passage, her mother muttering "If this is another of her lies . . ."

Poppy couldn't wait to see her face. Would she apologize for disbelieving her? Would she say, "Poppy, my dear love, I've misjudged you. Though you may tell the odd lie now and then, just to embroider a dull day, you can be trusted to tell the truth when it matters. I should've known!" Would she say that? Like hell! That'd be the day! Still, you never know! Perhaps—

She stopped short in the doorway, feeling the others crowding behind her. There was the chair in splintered pieces on the floor. There were the broken flowerpots. The water, left running, had overflowed the sink and was joining the earth on the floor in rivers of mud. But . . . no statue!

"It's gone! Where's it gone!" wailed Poppy.

"Well," said Mrs. Robbins, looking from the bewilderment on Poppy's face to the cold anger on her mother's. "Least said, soonest mended, I always say. Though that poor chair's 'ad it." She looked around with a practiced eye. "Fetch us a dustpan and brush, dearie. And them big bits can go straight in the bin. 'E'll never know they've gone."

Out in the passage a door closed softly, but none of them noticed. They were all too busy: Mrs. Robbins clearing up the mess, Mrs. Brown trying to control her anger, and Poppy getting ready to dodge, should her mother fail in this.

Out of sight, the stone creature waited.

4

Poppy, sent to bed without any supper, sat at her dressing table, brushing her damp hair. The unjust punishment did not trouble her. A book entitled *Proverbs, Saws and Sayings*, bought at a jumble sale for ten cents, had prepared her for life. "A liar's truth sounds as crooked as his tongue." "A wise man cares not for what he cannot have." (Such as supper.) Anyway, she wasn't hungry.

She studied her reflection earnestly. Why had the statue run away? Didn't it trust her? Did she really look . . . deceitful? Were her lies beginning to show in her face, as Foster-Mother Allen had warned her they would one day, after finding out that Poppy did not have a brother in reform school or a sister in Holloway Prison, but was an only child, trying to get sympathy under false pretenses.

She leaned nearer until, her nose resting on the cold glass, she saw the reflected eyes meet, touch corners, and become one long eye—like a Cyclops. A monster! Was that how everyone saw her? She moved back hastily, and her reflected face resumed its normal shape.

And where had *her* poor monster gone? Into the house . . . oh, heck! Slap bang into the middle of Mr. Hunt's treasures. For her mother's employer collected things, old things—the house was like a museum. All around, on every shelf, table, pedestal, and chest, there were heads.

Marble heads, bronze heads, heads in alabaster and heads in terracotta—and every one of them cut off below the neck! For a moment she seemed to see it through the statue's eyes—a butcher's shop! A chamber of horrors. A stone abattoir into which Poppy had led it. . . . She must explain. She must explain before it decided to remove *her* head from her shoulders, to keep on a mantelpiece between two brass candlesticks! And what about Mother Brown and Ma Robbins, who at any moment might blunder around a corner or open a cupboard . . . ?

She ran to the door and opened it—and there was Mrs. Robbins, smiling and winking, bringing a paper bag out of the bosom of her flowered apron.

"Brought you a bite of something to eat, you naughty girl," she whispered, "only don't let your ma—"

"I can't stop!" cried Poppy. "I've got to find it before—"

"Lost something, dearie? Never mind, it'll turn

up," said Mrs. Robbins, pushing Poppy back into the room. "Better not let your ma catch you out of 'ere, 'ad you? Or she'll lock you up next time, and you won't like that."

"But—but—" Poppy stammered, trying to explain the danger waiting somewhere in this house, behind the next corner or the next. . . . But now a vast flowery bosom filled her vision, so like a cushion for a tired head, and she longed to rest and be comforted. "It's frightened. It might . . . turn nasty," she said weakly.

It was no good. Mrs. Robbins seemed to think she was talking about a dog. She wasn't listening properly, having no time just now for Poppy's stories. Poppy found herself sitting on the bed, the paper bag in her lap.

"You tuck into that, dearie—and don't drop no crumbs what'll give me away."

"*What's that!*"

"A bit of cold chicken, love, and a slice of yer ma's pie what's still 'ot—"

"No! That *noise!*"

"I can't 'ear nothing. Only the wind and the rain."

"Listen!" said Poppy, going very pale. "Something's coming upstairs!"

" 'Ere, shove it under yer piller, quick!" Mrs. Robbins grabbed the bag herself and pushed it out of sight just in time. The door opened and Mrs. Brown came into the room, carrying a tray on which were a mug of milk and two Marie biscuits on a plate. Poppy was to be punished by missing her supper but not actually allowed to starve.

"I thought you'd gone home, Mrs. Robbins," Mrs. Brown said, for Mrs. Robbins lived down in the village with her husband and her cat, and only "helped out" during the day.

"Just going, dearie," Mrs. Robbins said hastily. "Night, Poppy, love. Night, Mrs. Brown."

"Good night!" Poppy called after her. "And Ma, —be careful! If you hear footsteps, don't look round, just *run!*"

"Don't call her Ma," said her mother, when the door had closed. "She's not your mother. I am."

She came across the room and put the tray on the bedside table. Then she stood, as if waiting for something.

"Thanks," muttered Poppy.

Still her mother stood there. What did she want? Could she smell the pie? Was the paper bag showing? Uneasily she turned her head to look—just as her mother bent down to kiss her. The kiss landed awkwardly on her left ear.

Mrs. Brown straightened up and walked quickly from the room, shutting the door behind her with a controlled slam.

That's torn it! thought Poppy. Now she thinks you've dodged her kiss on purpose. After she'd screwed herself up to it, too! You've been a disappointment again. Not only a liar, but unloving as well. Upsetting your poor mother. Making her ill. Why do you do everything wrong? Oh, well, if she needs another rest from you, Poppy Brown, who cares? There's plenty more mothers where she came from! Real, house, or foster, who cares? Rot 'em all!

She sat hugging herself as if she were cold, rocking backward and forward on her bed. Gradually her face, which had looked bleak, began to relax.

"Got to do something about Belladonna," she muttered.

For a long time she sat thinking. Then she grinned. Foster-Mother Mears! Foster-Mother Mears had had a stall selling "High-Fashion Jewelry" in a street market off Edgware Road. On Saturdays Poppy used to help. Now she remembered how Mother Mears always said, standing there with strings of beads dangling from her plump fingers, "Watch me, darling! It'll be an education. You gotta chat 'em up a bit, see? Put 'em in a good mood, crack a joke or two. Everyone loves a bit of glitter. Do it right and they'll be eating out of yer 'ands."

Taking a blanket from her bed, Poppy spread it out on the floor and placed in the middle four strings of beads, one butterfly brooch, one Snoopy badge, five safety pins, two plastic bangles, and a poster of Laurel and Hardy, rolled up and fastened with a rubber band.

She sat back on her heels and considered the

offering. It didn't glitter much, but it would have to do. It's the thought that counts, she reminded herself, tying the corners of the blanket together.

She crept out into the passage. It was dim and shadowy, lit only by a narrow window at the end. The house was quiet. Her room was in the servants' wing, a long way from the dining room below, where Mr. Hunt would be eating his slice of meat pie all alone. A long way from the kitchen where her mother would be eating her slice and diluting the gravy with her tears. The only sounds Poppy could hear were the rain at the window and the creaking of wooden boards (that might be only the old house settling on its foundation and not footsteps at all).

Please, Heaven, let Belladonna believe the heads and busts were made that way and not the result of human brutality! Let her love a bit of glitter. Don't let her crack my head open before I have a chance to speak.

5

Mr. Hunt's house was too large for him. Everyone knew this. In the past there would have been ten servants sleeping in the wing where now only Poppy and her mother slept. There would have been a large family to look after: children in the nursery, guests in the guest rooms, horses in the stables, and dogs everywhere. Not just one old, rich bachelor, his cook, and his cook's daughter.

"Crazy old hermit" was what they called Mr. Hunt in Charle, or so Mrs. Robbins reported. He took no interest in local affairs and seldom set foot in the village, though he would be seen driving through it in his big car on his way to an auction. That was all he cared about, his paintings, his china, and his statues. It was said he disliked company. Especially the company of children.

"It's very kind of him to let me have you here," her mother kept saying, "so you be good." Don't make so much noise. Don't go into his part of the house. Don't play in front of his windows. Use the back door, the back stairs, the second-best tea set! It's very kind of him to let you live here, Poppy. It's very kind of him to let you breathe, so try not to do it so loudly!

Poppy had only met him face to face once, when she had first arrived at Charle House. He had welcomed her, shaking her hand and calling her Miss Brown, which had made her giggle and her mother blush for her. Since then she had only seen him in the distance, and she did not think he had noticed her at all. That was fine. That was the way she wanted to keep it.

But there was only the drawing room left to search and that was next to the study. She stood wearily at the end of the kitchen passage, looking across the shadowy main hall to where the line of light showed under the study door. He would be sitting in his leather chair, sipping his brandy and reading his book and safely out of the way for the next couple of hours. There was no reason why he should come out to find her creeping like a thief across his Persian rugs, with his best red blanket slung over her shoulder. Was there?

As she moved forward, her bundle caught on something. She looked down; it was the handle of the cellar door.

She opened it, switched on the light, and gazed down the stairs. On the fifth step down there was something small and thin and green. Grass green.

It was in fact a blade of grass stuck to the step with mud. The mud was not quite dry.

Poppy's heart began to hammer. The cellars ran right underneath the house. Even on such a hot evening, the air was cool and damp, and smelled of coal and dust and earth. The light was dim, and the corners gray with cobwebs and shadows. Only the first cellar was wired for light or ever swept.

Poppy went slowly down the stairs, past the rows of wine racks, until she came to the archway leading to the cellars beyond. A little light spilled forward onto the unswept floor. There in the dust, quite plain, she saw the print of a naked foot.

She stopped. Her proverbs jostled nervously in her mind, seeming to contradict each other. Discretion is the better part of valor. On the other hand, he who hesitates is lost. Then again, look before you leap. It's a wise child, she thought in some confusion, who goes no farther. Certainly nothing was going to make her venture into the dark without even a candle to be blown out.

"Belladonna!" she called softly, and heard the echo's hesitant reply.

"Honor, honor!"

Then silence, except for water dripping somewhere.

"I have a present for you!"

"You, you, you."

"It's a nice present. More than one! Lots of

pretty things! And a mirror. Won't you come and see? I won't hurt you. I'm your friend."

"End, end, end."

Silence again. Then there was an odd click, followed by a low humming, as if the central heating had just come on. Nothing else.

"Well, if you don't want them, I'll take them away."

Then it came. The answer.

A terrible sound! Harsh, grinding, inhuman. Like a stone door opening, letting out pain and anger. . . . Poppy trembled and the bundle dropped from her fingers to the ground, raising a small explosion of dust. Even the echo stuttered in alarm.

Then it came again, the stone shouting.

She hesitated no longer. Her legs knew what to do and they did it. They carried her at high speed through the wine cellar, up the steep stairs, and through the door. Then they began to shake at the knees. She shut the door, turned the key, and sank down on to the floor, unable to stand a moment longer.

Coward! she accused herself. You're nothing but a miserable little coward, Poppy Brown. But she made no effort to return to the cellar and was quite content to sit on the floor, with her back against the door, staring down at the rug in front of her.

One brown, highly polished shoe stepped on to the rug. Then another one. She looked up, saw first a pair of trousered legs, then a brown velvet smoking jacket, and then at the very top, Mr. Hunt's head.

He was a tall man, thin, in spite of her mother's cooking, and wispy. The hair of his eyebrows grew straight up and showed in tall tufts above his glasses like vegetation forcing its way out of a green house. His hair was thick and gray, with the same tendency to grow in odd directions. His eyes were hidden by the light reflecting on his glasses.

She stared up at him, unable to speak.

"Ah—it's Miss Brown, isn't it? Ah—good evening," he said.

She couldn't answer.

"I just came—ah—for some more brandy," he said, after a pause. "I didn't want to disturb your mother so I thought I'd—ah—fetch it myself."

"No!"

"No? But, my dear young lady, why ever not?" he asked, looking at her in bewilderment.

"Just . . . don't! Please! Not tonight!"

There was a silence, during which Mr. Hunt stared at her, his eyebrows risen quite clear of his glasses, while Poppy hung her head and hid her face in her long hair. She was trying to think of a convincing lie but her wits seemed to have deserted her.

"I've only had one glass of brandy," Mr. Hunt said finally. "The bottle's empty and I want another bottle—and you're sitting in front of the door."

Poppy did not move.

"I usually have *two* glasses of brandy," he went on, beginning to sound annoyed. "No more. I assure you I'm quite accustomed to two glasses and—" He stopped, remembering he was talking to a child. Poppy did not look up. "Is your mother a teetotaler?" he asked.

"I don't know."

There was another pause.

"Isn't it time you were in bed?" he asked hopefully.

She didn't answer.

With a great creaking of knees, he came down to her level and tried to see her face through her soft, mouse-brown hair.

"Why mayn't I go into my own cellar?" he asked plaintively.

"There's—there's something in there."

"What sort of thing?"

Should she tell him the truth? No. He'd never believe it.

"A—a mad dog." It was the best she could do, and not very good.

"A dog?" repeated Mr. Hunt, puzzled. He did not own a dog. "Is it Mr. Shepherd's dog? Is it Fido? If it's got shut in, the poor animal's probably frightened, that's all." He took Poppy gently but firmly by the arm and helped her to her feet. "Now you run off to bed and leave it to me, young lady."

He tried to open the door, found it locked, unlocked it, and went down the stairs. Poppy watched him from the doorway. He looked about him, saw nothing unusual, and then walked toward the dark archway.

The bundle had gone! In the short time they'd been talking, it had been taken away! Poppy opened her mouth to shout a warning but her tongue seemed to have turned to stone.

Mr. Hunt stood in the archway, looking very thin and old and breakable.

"Fido!" he called. "Fido! Fido!"

And the echo answered. "Hide, oh hide, o!"

Good advice, thought Poppy. He was no match for Belladonna. She found her voice.

"Come back! There wasn't a dog at all!" she shouted.

Mr. Hunt turned and looked up at her.

"A joke!" she said feebly.

When she was quite certain he was coming, clutching his bottle of brandy, she ducked around the corner out of sight. She heard him come out of the cellar. There was a pause, while he was probably looking around for her, and then the sound of his footsteps retreating toward his study. A door opening and a door closing. He had gone.

Poppy crept around the corner and turned the key in the lock. It was the only door into the cellar. It was a very stout door. She thought it would hold. She removed the key and put it in her pocket.

"Got you!" she said, and went to bed.

6

Night came. Only a rat heard the noises in the cellar and fled in terror. The three sleepers above turned restlessly but did not wake. Then the sun rose in a white haze, birds began to sing, and Poppy's alarm clock went off. It was six o'clock.

Her first thought was of the statue. In her sleep-muddled head it seemed like a dream. Perhaps it had been one. Then she wouldn't have to get out of her warm bed and go down to the dark cellar. . . . But then why had she set the alarm? She lay and thought about it. She fell asleep.

By afternoon the haze had cleared and it was blazing hot outside. The fat girl's face shone like an apple. Poppy felt like biting it.

"I'm sorry," said the fat girl, "I didn't mean to get you into trouble, but how was I to know it wasn't true?"

Poppy did not answer. On the far side of the lawn, Mr. Shepherd, the gardener, was bending over a shrub. Although it was possible he had not seen her, Poppy felt he had turned his back on her. He was not her friend.

"I mean—I don't care if he isn't your uncle. It's nothing to me either way," said the fat girl. "I can't think why you said he was—unless you were trying to impress me? Not that Mr. Hunt is anyone special; he's rich, that's all. Are you ashamed of your mother being a cook? Are you a snob or something?"

Mr. Hunt had played many roles in Poppy's recent lies. Now an uncle, now the head of a gang of art thieves, even a murderer who hid the dismembered pieces of victims among his collection, having first covered them with clay and baked them in the oven. Once she had claimed him as her "illegitimate father" and felt uneasy when people had laughed and stared and whispered together. Please Heaven that one never came back to her mother!

"It was a joke," she said.

"A joke! Oh, well, ha ha!" The fat girl looked slyly at Poppy. "Your mother didn't seem amused. You do tell some rather peculiar jokes, don't you?"

"If you mean I'm a liar, why don't you say so?"

Fido lifted his head at the sound of their voices. After a moment he put his nose back on his paws and shut his eyes, as if Poppy were a black sheep not worth collecting.

The fat girl said, "I don't know why I bother

with you. You're as prickly as a hedgehog. Look, a few lies don't worry me."

Poppy looked at her without enthusiasm. The fat girl's name was Emma Hodge. All last term Poppy had been keeping her at arm's length. Being a child of nearly as many new schools as new mothers, she had grown to be suspicious of those girls who seemed too eager to make friends. She had noticed that Emma was always one of the last two to be chosen to make up a side. The other one of course was Poppy herself, but then she was the new girl. It was a mistake to link oneself to someone who was unpopular. A man is judged by the company he keeps. But today, having no other friends, not even a statue, she relented a little.

"Then try this one," she said. "What do you think those are?" She pointed to the ugly dark marks that stretched across the lawn toward the shrubbery on the far side.

"They look like footsteps, only they're too deep."

"They are footsteps."

"Giants?" asked Emma. She tried to fit her fat foot in its sensible brown sandal into the nearest hole; it was the wrong shape. Although shorter, it was too wide to go in. "No, not a giant."

"A statue," said Poppy.

The fat girl looked at her and then crouched down and examined the hole carefully. It was shaped very like a footprint, although it had little instep and you couldn't see the separate toes.

It was between one and two inches deep, with fairly clear-cut edges. Emma stood up again and stamped her foot hard on the grass. The grass rose again almost immediately. There was no print. She looked thoughtfully at the other holes; they were about the right distance for a longish stride.

She said, "I believe you."

"Nobody else did," Poppy said bitterly. "They just blamed me. All of them. Old Shep"—she indicated the distant gardener—"Mother Brown, of course. Even Ma Robbins. And no doubt Mr. Hunt will, only he's gone off to an auction."

"How did they think you did it?"

"That's what I asked them. And they couldn't think—until old Shep said it must've been my pogo stick. They all believed *him*. Right away. Even though I've *never* been able to go more than one jump on it without falling over!"

"A pogo stick would've left a round hole."

"My very words! But Mother Brown said it would've rocked forward under my weight and—and elongated it."

Emma shook her head. "No. I thought of that. It would've left a different-shaped mark. Wider at the top and narrow at the bottom. These are the same all the way down."

Poppy remembered that the fat girl, however unpopular, was always top of the class.

"Is there any other evidence?" Emma asked.

Poppy led her through the shrubbery to the little

neglected garden and showed her the empty pedestal. It was stained with a greenish mold in places and lightly discolored all over, so that the two whitish patches where the statue's feet had been showed up plainly.

"What did they say about this?"

"Mother Brown and Ma Robbins said it wasn't no use them going blundering about in a lot of nasty wet bushes. Never having been there before, how could they know if there's been a statue there in the first place—getting their feet wet for nothing!"

"But Mr. Shepherd! He must've known! Not that it looks as if he did much gardening around here—" said Emma, looking at the tangled grass and weeds. "Still, didn't he say anything?"

"He said a lot. He went on and on saying it. For ages! But it's no good asking me. He has such an accent, I never understand more than one word in four. Which is more than Mother Brown—she doesn't understand him at *all!*"

Emma laughed. "What's that?" she asked, pointing to a dark mark close to a deep crack in the stone. It had a faint greenish-black metallic gleam.

Poppy explained about the bracelet. She told Emma everything that had happened. Yesterday was easy. Today was more difficult to explain.

"You mean, you've done nothing? Just left it locked up in the cellar?" asked Emma, staring.

"Well . . ." said Poppy, feeling guilty. She supposed she should have done something. Only it was so hot. The sun felt like a weight on the top of her head, and the statue felt like a weight at the bottom of her mind. It was all too much for her.

Emma, who was now sitting cross-legged on the pedestal, like a Buddha, looked at her in silence. A round face is less expressive than a thin one. Poppy had no idea what she was thinking.

"Do you believe me?" she challenged.

"I believe you," said Emma. "On Thursdays I believe everything. It's my believing day."

"Will you believe me tomorrow?"

Emma grinned and shook her head. "I doubt it. A bit too fantastic for a Friday, I'm afraid."

So she had never really believed her at all! What a sly, horrid beast she was! She probably couldn't wait to tell them all next term, and then—Poppy could see it already—the little groups of girls who stopped talking when she approached, the exchanged glances, the giggles smothered behind hands, fingers tapping foreheads significantly. . . . She'd never live it down.

Unless she got in first? *She* could be the center of that giggling group if she played her cards right. Let's see—do you know why old Podge is so fat? It's because she swallows everything she's told! Emma would find out two could play that game!

But what a dirty game it was, she thought, ashamed. Why had she ever let Emma into her secret garden? She looked around sadly. With the grass crushed and tumbled, the statue gone, and Emma on the pedestal, it was not the same. She felt it would never be the same again.

"I wish I'd never brought you here," she said.

"Was this your special place?" asked Emma, looking around. "Have I spoiled it for you? I'm sorry." She got awkwardly off the pedestal and stood looking at Poppy. "I didn't mean I thought you were lying. Only . . . it's a bit, well . . ."

"I suppose you'll tell them all."

"Who?"

"At school."

"Of course not! What do you take me for? We're friends now, aren't we? *Aren't we?*" Emma repeated as Poppy hesitated. "Why are you always so—so stand-offish? Don't you want to be friends? It's not as if you had any other friends yet."

"Nor have *you.*"

Emma stared at her, her face crimsoning.

"So that's it! I see it all now! You think I'm a reject, some sort of—of leper—that's why you've been holding back! Afraid of being contaminated if you're seen talking to me, I suppose? What a nasty, calculating, cold-blooded little rat you are! To think I was sorry for you! Do you always judge people by their pop rating? Let me tell you, you little toad, I may not have many friends but I'd be ashamed to number you among them! So you needn't worry! *Good-bye!*"

She pushed through the bushes and was gone.

Poppy sat in her ruined garden and began to cry. Was she really horrid? she wondered, feeling uneasily it might be true. When a friend asks, there is no tomorrow, she thought gloomily. A friend is not so soon gotten as lost. Make not thy friend thy foe. A friend is another self. There was no comfort in her proverbs. They all seemed to confirm that what she had rejected was beyond price. But it was too late.

The bushes rustled and Emma came back.

"I thought I'd give you one more chance," she said, scowling. "For your sake, it's not that *I* care one way or the other. So don't think you'd be doing me a favor, because it's the other way around. Well?"

"I'd like to be friends," Poppy said humbly. Make it go well this time, she thought, make it last.

Emma Hodge beamed. "Good," she said. "Now we can search your cellar."

7

It was impossible to feel nervous when Emma was so obviously enjoying herself. Did Poppy have a flashlight? she asked. Poppy had two flashlights, but neither of them worked anymore. Never mind. Emma unscrewed the handsome new lamp from her bicycle. Did Poppy have a camera and a flash attachment? No? Never mind. Did Poppy have a bag to carry any evidence they might discover?

"Yes," said Poppy, glad to have something.

She followed Emma down the cellar stairs, past the wine racks to the dark archway beyond.

"I'd better go first as I've got the lamp," said Emma.

Poppy agreed. She was not going to be so selfish as to insist on being the heroine.

"I'm right behind you," she said.

Emma switched on her lamp. The pale circle of light moved through the dark like a fastidious moon through a dirty sky; past clouds of cobwebs, across walls now black with damp, now green with mold, showing here an abandoned sofa with its stuffing oozing out, there old kettles without lids, pans without handles, dust, everywhere dust—and footprints in the dust.

Emma squatted down and examined one closely. Then, as if by accident, the light moved sideways till it shone on Poppy's feet.

"No. Not mine," said Poppy. She removed her sandal and trod carefully in the dust. The light moved from her print to the other and back again.

"No," said Emma, sounding puzzled. Poppy's print showed a deeply curved instep and small toes like round islands, separated from the ball of the foot. The alien print was straight-sided, widening to the top like a partly opened fan and ending in a scalloped edge. There was a chip out of the left heel as if a piece had broken off.

"Flat-footed, isn't she?" said Poppy.

The light moved to shine briefly in Poppy's face, as if hoping to surprise the sly grin of someone playing a practical joke. She doesn't really believe me, thought Poppy. It's just a game to her.

They went on. Dust. Footprints. Something pale . . . A face! Caught in the light, a fat face smiled happily up at them from the floor. It was torn off at the neck.

"My poster! My Laurel and Hardy Poster! What did she have to tear it up for?" cried Poppy.

Emma swung the light over the floor. The poster was ripped into pieces. Red beads lay scattered in the dust like drops of blood. The Snoopy badge and the butterfly brooch were crushed almost beyond recognition.

"What did she want to do that for?" Poppy whispered.

There was something horrible about the destruction of her gift. A senseless fury which made the cellar seem colder and darker and full of menace. No noise from the house reached them there. There was only the sound of their own breathing and water dripping somewhere out of sight.

"Let's go back," Poppy whispered.

The light trembled in Emma's hand. She did not answer. Perhaps she was too frightened to move. Poppy could understand that; she was too frightened to move herself. She wished she were out of the cellar, upstairs, anywhere, but the thought of taking one more step through the dark that smelled of dust and things rotting quietly in forgotten corners . . . She did not even know which way she was facing. Had she turned around?

The light was moving.

"Emma!"

"Look! It got out," said Emma, shining her lamp into the next cellar. Poppy joined her.

There was a yellow patch of sunlight on the floor, so bright that it made the light from the bicycle lamp look as if it were taking ill. It glinted on the clean edges of the broken glass that lay on the floor. Poppy looked up. Practically all the glass had gone from the grating, except for a ragged fringe around the sides. The iron bars had been forced apart so violently that one had come completely away from the stonework and now lay in the broken glass at their feet.

She must've gone mad down here, Poppy thought uneasily, looking at the twisted bars. She must've been desperate. She was used to the open air. I shouldn't have locked her in! No wonder she tore up my gifts.

Aloud she said, "I'm *glad* she got away from this filthy old cellar! She's so pretty."

She turned to Emma. The sunlight from the grating fell upon Emma's face. There was a large smudge of dirt on her cheek and a smaller one on her nose and her dark hair looked dusty. There couldn't have been a greater contrast between her and the pale, pretty statue. Perhaps something in Poppy's expression gave away this thought, for Emma's face went wooden. She started walking back without saying anything. Poppy caught her up.

"I suppose I'll have to go on looking for her. I mean . . . she's my friend," she said, not improving matters.

"Some friend."

"It's just . . . if she's frightened, she might be dangerous. If only I can explain—"

"Why are you calling it 'she'? You called it 'it' before," said Emma.

"I dunno. After all, it was the statue of a girl."

"It *was*. What is it now? A monster!"

Poppy sighed. It had been much easier having a statue as a friend. People were so touchy.

Outside it was very hot. The air was not as fresh as they might have hoped, but seemed to taste slightly of curry, even when they were some distance from the kitchen. The statue was not in the garden. They looked everywhere, behind every bush and hedge, examined every path and flowerbed. Finally they arrived hot and tired at the end of the drive.

Poppy looked down the road to the village and up the road to the moors. Nothing was in sight.

"Which way d'you think?"

"What was she wearing?" asked Emma.

"A sort of stone scarf around her hips. Nothing else. Unless she's wearing a red blanket!"

"If she's gone to the village, she'll certainly be noticed," said Emma.

Poppy smiled, glad Emma had come out of her sulks.

"What's up the other way?" Poppy asked. "Just the moors?"

She was a town child, not overfond of walking for its own sake, and had always chosen to go down to the village, where at least there was a shop that sold candy and postcards. Looking up the road, she had no idea what was around the corner. Now it seemed extraordinary that she had never bothered to find out.

"If you take the right fork, about two miles up, that's the way to Boverley," Emma told her. "The other way goes straight up to the moors, past Forster's—"

"Forster's?"

"You know, that big place that sells urns and garden furniture and statues. . . ."

Emma stopped and they stared at each other.

"I bet that's where she is," said Poppy. "Come on!"

"Poppy, it's *miles*! And uphill all the way. It would take well over an hour and I'm already late for my tea."

Poppy stared up the hill. The sun blazed down on her head. Miles! If only they had a car, if only people would believe her, they could be driven up there in a few minutes. . . .

"Everyone knows I'm a liar, that's the trouble," she said. She looked thoughtfully at Emma. "I suppose *you* couldn't tell them?"

Emma looked embarrassed. "I couldn't actually say I'd seen her come to life—well, could I? I mean, I didn't. And I'm no good at lying. I always blush."

"I never blush," said Poppy. "Perhaps if I had, I wouldn't have gone on telling lies." But for a thick skin and a lazy blood supply, she could have been as virtuous as Emma. It seemed unfair. "I'm going to turn over a new leaf," she said. "I'm going to learn to blush and get myself a good reputation. You'll see. I'll stop lying—" Remembering the lady of Devizes, she raised her hand in the air and said, "May God strike me dead if I ever tell another lie!"

Immediately there came a low mutter of thunder. The girls looked up into the clear blue sky and then at one another in dismay.

"You've done it now!" said Emma. "Quick, tell Him you didn't mean it!"

"How can I?"

"Go on! Kneel down and tell Him—tell Him you just meant you'd *try* not to. Go on. I won't laugh! I won't tell anyone, ever. Honest, Poppy."

"I can't," said Poppy, embarrassed. "Supposing someone comes? Anyway, I'm not sure whether— do *you* believe in God?"

"I don't know," Emma said uneasily, keeping her voice down. "Sometimes."

"Oh, well, a bargain is a bargain," said Poppy, trying to sound unconcerned. "I'll just have to be careful."

"No one can be *that* careful," said Emma.

On the way back to the house, Emma kept looking at Poppy, almost as if she were trying to memorize her face in case Poppy died in the night. It began to make Poppy nervous. She crossed her fingers—but she couldn't keep her fingers crossed for the rest of her life. Was it too late to tell God she'd changed her mind? She did not know. Religion was a muddle. Mother Brown's God, she knew, was stern, full of vengeance and fury, and already angry with her for her wicked lies. But other mothers had seemed shocked when she told them this, called her a poor child, and told her that God was love.

That night Poppy lay in bed, holding her old teddy she had dug out of the bottom of the wardrobe. She had felt in need of comfort.

I'm doomed to an early death, she told it. Sooner or later someone will ask me if I like her new dress, and I'll forget and say yes just to be polite. And that'll be it! The end of poor Poppy Brown! Struck down dead.

She wondered if they would erect a monument. Turning to face the wall, she began counting, instead of sheep, the people who might weep at her funeral. Unfortunately she ran out of people long before she fell asleep.

Outside, in the dark sky, the storm gathered.

8

In the churchyard at Boverley, an owl hooted twice. A small black cat came out from between two gravestones. It was thin and young, and frightened. This night was strange indeed! The cat could hear dogs growling in the sky. Its fur prickled and would not lie flat, as if invisible hands brushed it the wrong way. Now and then a claw of blinding light ripped apart the dark sky. It was no night for a young cat to be out.

It ran quickly down the path toward the church porch, stopped and peered with its domed eyes into the deeper shadows within. A figure was standing there.

The young cat, always hopeful, always hungry, walked toward this figure, uttering the most pitiful cries. It stopped. Its nose twitched a warning. Wrong smell. The hair stood upright on its arched back and it spat.

At that moment lightning forked out of the clouds and everything was lit with unnatural brilliance. The little cat hesitated, then fled past the pale figure into the shelter of the porch and crouched trembling as thunder crashed outside. In the churchyard a stone angel tilted, seemed to hang for a moment, and then fell sideways onto the path, sending up a shower of small stones that pattered down upon it with a noise like hail.

Now the figure moved stiffly out of the porch. The cat crept forward and stared, its eyes bulging. It saw the figure help the fallen angel to its feet. They stood there, side by side, now lit by lightning to a sudden white, now hardly visible even to the cat's night eyes. There was a sound of low humming. Rain began to fall heavily. The two pale figures turned and walked through the wet grass, making the earth tremble. Then they were out of sight.

The little cat backed away from the rain and went to sit under the seat on the right side of the porch, where someone had left a warm woolen blanket. It began to wash itself vigorously.

"You're very quiet, dearie," said Mrs. Robbins, looking at Poppy as she sat drooping over her cornflakes. "Cat got your tongue, then?"

"She's been very quiet ever since she got up," said Mrs. Brown. "I think she's coming down with something. I don't think you ought to go on a picnic today," she told her daughter. "Sitting about in the hot sun won't do you any good when you're not feeling well."

"I am feeling well. I don't think I'm coming down with anything. I do want to go on the picnic," Poppy said carefully.

Her mother stared at her. "Why are you talking funnily? Have you got a sore throat?"

"No."

" 'Oo are you going with?" asked Mrs. Robbins.

"Emma Hodge."

"Well now! Very nice, too. I know the 'Odges. Mrs. Court does for 'em. Lovely place they 'ave, she says. Where're you going, then?"

"We thought we'd take the road to the moors."

"That's nice," said Mrs. Robbins. "Not that I fancy 'em meself. Lonely. No people. Nowhere to get a cuppa. I always think, what if someone 'ad an accident? Fell down and broke a leg? 'Oo'd 'ear them call for help? Still," she added, "they say it's very pretty, if that's the sorta thing you like."

Mrs. Brown looked worried.

"Don't go and get lost!" she said sharply. "Perhaps it isn't a good idea. It's a wild sort of place, from what I've heard."

"Oh, please!" said Poppy.

"They won't come to no 'arm," said Mrs. Robbins, trying to make amends. "Emma 'Odge is a sensible girl. Born and bred in the village. She'll know the moors like the back of 'er 'and."

"It's t'feet, noan t'hands. Luke where tha poots t'feet," said the gardener bafflingly. "Lest tha fall doon t'hole. There's t'owd mines opp there. Never barded opp, ther worn't."

Mrs. Brown looked unhappy. This was her first job up North, and she had not yet understood one word the old man said, so thick was his accent. She did not want to offend him by asking him to repeat himself all the time. Besides, it was no good; his second version was just as incomprehensible.

"More tea?" she asked, guessing wildly. "Yes, of course. I'll just hot it up a little."

She picked up the teapot and moved over to the stove. Mrs. Robbins winked at Poppy, and leaning over, whispered a rough translation.

" 'E says there's old mines up there that 'aven't been boarded up proper, so you'll be careful, won't you, dearie?"

Poppy nodded.

"Well, 'adn't you better be off, then?" Mrs. Robbins went on, raising her voice. "Else you'll miss the bus." By which she meant only that Poppy should take the chance of going while her mother's back was turned.

"There's noan bouss goan t'moors," said Mr. Shepherd.

"It's just coming," said Mrs. Brown, meaning the tea.

Now she *had* offended him. He had lived in Charle all his life and here was this newcomer, this foreigner, contradicting him. There'd never been a bus along this road, not in his own time, nor his father's before him.

"There's noan buoss goan t'moors," he said angrily. "Tha daft owd witch!"

"*What* did he say?" Mrs. Brown asked suspiciously.

" 'E said something about digging a ditch," Mrs. Robbins said tactfully.

The gardener got up, muttering to himself, and went out into the garden. Then he opened the door again and beckoned to Poppy. Surprised, she followed him outside. What had she done wrong now? He led her toward a large shed, told her to wait outside while he went inside, and came out wheeling a bicycle.

"There's noan buoss goan oop t'moors," he said. "Tha'd best tek this 'un, lass."

"You mean—I can borrow it? Really?" Poppy exclaimed happily. She had always longed for a bicycle, but Mother Brown said they could not afford it. Today they had been going to take turns on Emma's, which had five gears and a mirror on the handlebars. This one was old and did not seem to have any gears at all, but Poppy was delighted with it. "Thank you! I'll take good care of it," she promised.

"T'maister'll never miss 'un," said Mr. Shepherd.

Poppy had misjudged him. His warning about the mines must have been kindly meant. Half an hour later, she changed her mind again. It would have been easier to walk up the hill without having to push a heavy old bicycle.

"Is it uphill *all* the way?" she asked.

"Yes. But it's lovely coming down," Emma said, to comfort her.

"The brakes probably don't work. How much farther is it to the statue place?"

"Two miles. Two and a half, perhaps."

"As much as that! I can't possibly—" She broke off. "I think I will find it very tiring to complete the journey," she finished carefully.

Emma looked puzzled at first, then laughed. "Oh, are you speaking the truth? It does sound peculiar. But you needn't bother. I asked Mike." (Mike was her brother who always passed his tests and was known to be a genius.) "He says you needn't worry about God striking you dead."

"Why not?"

"He doesn't believe in God. He says it's all superstition."

"Oh," Poppy said doubtfully. She *was* superstitious. She never walked under ladders and was always touching wood. "I think I'll play safe," she decided.

A farm truck came rattling down the road, slowing down as it passed them. The driver stuck his head out of the window, shouted something, waved, and drove on.

"What did he say?"

"Something about an angel, I think," said Emma, shrugging.

"An *angel?*"

"Perhaps he thought you looked like one."

"Ha! Ha!"

Then a youth on a bicycle came sweeping around the corner. He too slowed down when he saw them.

"Haven't seen an angel walking about, has tha?" he called.

"What?"

"T'vicar's gone and lost an angel. Over at Boverley. . . ." His voice floated back to them as he released his brakes. "Out of t'graveyard. Big stone 'un with great wings. Done a flit!"

They could hear his laughter diminishing down the hill till he was out of sight.

"Emma! Emma, it can't be a coincidence, can it? It thundered during the night. I woke up and heard it."

"But there've been storms every summer, Poppy. And nothing's ever happened before."

"It's that chain," Poppy said slowly, beginning to walk on. "I meant to tell you, only I forgot, what with getting this bike. You know the bracelet I told you about? The one I gave Belladonna?"

"The one the lightning struck?"

"Yes. I made it out of some old chains I found in the cellar. It was in a funny old pot with rude pictures on it. There's a lot—"

"Rude pictures?" asked Emma interested.

"Oh, you know—naked women and men with goat's legs, that sort of thing."

"Oh, is that all," said Emma, disappointed.

"I only took a short piece of chain that was lying on top," Poppy went on. "But there was plenty more. It was a big pot and it was nearly full."

"What about it? I mean, was it special in any way?"

"I don't know. It was an odd color, a sort of greeny black. And it looked very old. And it's *gone*! I looked this morning before breakfast. The pot's still there but it's empty. The chain has all gone. Belladonna must've taken it."

9

Forster's was surrounded by a high wall of black-ened stone, above which only the tops of trees showed. On either side the moors rolled away into the distance, khaki-colored under the hot sun. Here and there a lump of gray stone stood out of the short dry grass, leaning wistfully toward Forster's, as if ambitious to become a statue in somebody's cool garden.

"No one could climb over those walls," said Poppy. "It looks like a prison."

The tall, wrought-iron gates, however, were standing wide open.

"Do they lock them at night, d'you think?"

"The padlock looks new," said Emma. "I expect they do. Mike says their stuff is good. Mostly antique. They buy it up from big old houses when they're demolished. Mike says there used to be a lot of rich mine owners around here and . . ."

Poppy stopped listening. She had never met

Mike but she was already a little tired of him. He was always creeping into Emma's conversation. She looked across the wide courtyard toward the house. Smaller than she had expected, it looked as if it was considering whether or not to become a ruin. Most of the windows on the first floor were cracked or broken and not even boarded up. The ground-floor windows, though undamaged, were so grimy that she could not see through them. There was a truck parked on the right, with its tailboard down, forming a ramp. Beside this was a low metal cart, on which was a human shape, done up in sacking and tied up with rope.

She nudged Emma, pointing to it.

"Mr. Forster, I presume?"

There was nobody in sight. The short flight of steps to the open front door was guarded by two massive stone lions, with their mouths wide open, as if showing some invisible dentist that they had several broken teeth. There were also two bronze greyhounds, a couple of small, chipped dragons, and a hybrid creature that was half woman, half beast and wholly horrible.

"I hope your Belladonna doesn't set this lot free," whispered Emma.

"Perhaps she already has. Perhaps that's why the place is deserted. They've already done in the Forsters, and now they're just sitting there, waiting for us. Go and touch one and see if it bites! I dare you!"

Emma hesitated, then walked over and patted a lion on its head.

"*What are you doing? Leave it alone!*" shouted an angry voice.

Both girls jumped. From behind the truck came a very large man with a weatherbeaten face and thick, curly gray hair, followed by an equally tall but younger edition of himself.

"We just wanted to look around," said Poppy.

"Be off with you!" the older man said crossly.

"'Ee, Father, it's nobbut two pretty young lassies," the younger one said, smiling at them. "They'll do no harm."

"Lassies or lads, they're all the same nowadays. Hooligans! Vandals, the lot of 'em! Carve their initials on the Venus de Milo, they would," said the older man, scowling. "No respect for other people's property—"

"Now that's a thought, Father," said his son. "It must be the two as took the vicar's angel. Six foot tall, she were. Weighed near a ton, I shouldn't wonder. Best turn your pockets out, miss. The vicar'd like his angel back."

His father was not amused.

"If your ma hadn't sworn you were home all night," he said, staring at his son suspiciously, "I know where my eyes 'ud be looking. I know which way my finger'd point." He put out a large red forefinger and tapped his son on the chest. "That were a block-and-tackle job all right. And who's got a block and tackle in these parts? Forster's, that's who. *Us.* I know *I* didn't do it. I know your ma didn't do it. That leaves—"

"Not me, Father," said his son, grinning widely.

"It isn't funny, lad. The poor vicar . . . . He! He! He!" His face suddenly creased into laughter, "Well, maybe it is, at that! But if you had any hand in it, you'd best own up."

The young man shook his curly head. "Never saw an angel in my life. Not till I met you, miss," he said, smiling at Poppy; then catching sight of Emma, he added politely, "And you, miss."

"I'm too fat for an angel," said Emma.

"Angels come in all sizes," old Mr. Forster said kindly. He had been a fat boy in his youth and still remembered the teasing. "You're nice and cuddly, lass. You're none too fat."

Emma smiled at him brilliantly. Poppy, watching, thought with surprise that she looked almost pretty.

Softened by his own kindly feelings, Mr. Forster gave them permission to look around the grounds.

"Only no damage," he warned them. "No carving initials, now."

They promised.

"Give us a call when you're leaving," he said. "We don't want to lock you in for the night—"

"You do lock the gates at night, then?" asked Poppy.

"Why? Why do you want to know?"

"Just wondered."

"We lock the gates at six o'clock," old Mr. Forster said slowly, suspiciously. "And we let Rex and Tarzan off their leads. You tell your friends that, young lady. We'll have no . . . jokes . . . here, thank you."

He turned abruptly and walked into the house. His son, winking at the girls, followed him.

"You shouldn't have said that. You've made him suspicious," said Emma as they threaded their way through a collection of vast stone urns. "Now he'll remember you."

"He'd remember me anyway," said Poppy. "I hope I'm not so easily forgotten. Still, if Belladonna's here, we'd better find her before she gets busy with that chain."

But it was not going to be easy. The grounds at the back of the house were divided, by hedges and evergreens and ivy-covered trellises, into innumerable small gardens, so that customers could wander from one to another and appreciate the different effects. Here was a square lawn on which a bronze dancer held his ballerina aloft, so improbably balanced that it seemed she must fall at any moment. Next they found themselves in a formal garden, surrounded by dark yew hedges. In the middle a small stone boy rode a dolphin and smiled down at the goldfish in the pond below. Four stone women, one at each corner, stood watching.

"The Four Seasons," said Emma knowledgeably.

The one nearest Poppy was holding sheaves of corn. Autumn, she supposed. She poked it with her finger. The stone felt hard, rough, unchanged. She looked down. There was no chain on its ankles. "Belladonna hasn't been here," she said thankfully. Then she looked sharply over her shoulder. "What was that?" she asked.

"What?"

"I thought something moved."

"Can't see anything."

The next garden was crowded with stone children. Some held flowers in their hands, some bowls of fruit, while others clasped large fish to their fat stomachs, looking around uncertainly as if wondering where their ponds had gone. Many had wings on their shoulders, too small to lift a good-sized duck, let alone a fat stone cherub. The one in the middle was riding a goat, garlanded with flowers. Under a mass of grapelike curls, his eyes slitted in eternal laughter.

"I love him!" Poppy declared. "He's sweet— even if his nose is slightly chipped. Poor little cherub. . . . Lend me your bracelet."

"Why?"

"For Chipnose." She patted the boy's stone curls affectionately. "Wouldn't you rather have him and his goat than a bracelet? We could put it around the goat's leg—"

"No!" said Emma, not certain whether Poppy

was joking. "Daddy gave it to me for my birthday. It's silver."

"Oh, well, it probably wouldn't work then," said Poppy, shrugging her shoulders and walking on. "Probably it has to be that special chain—" She broke off. "Can you hear anything?" she asked.

"No. Only that humming."

"What is it? Bees?"

"Sounds mechanical. Perhaps they have electric hoists and things."

They walked on. Four more Seasons, a shepherd and shepherdess, a Hercules, a winged Mercury. Statue after statue, but no Belladonna. No angels. It was very hot. Once or twice a plane flew overhead or a noisy bumblebee droned past; otherwise it was quiet. The humming had stopped. Emma began to get bored. She was famished, she said.

They sat down by a small pond, in the shade of a huge Father Neptune, and ate their lunch.

Poppy kept glancing over her shoulder.

"What's the matter?" Emma asked.

"I don't know," said Poppy. "It's just, I keep thinking I see something out of the corner of my eye but when I look, there's nothing there. I keep feeling there's someone watching us. Perhaps it's the goldfish."

She rolled over onto her stomach and began feeding her sandwich to the fish.

Not liking to see good food wasted, Emma got up and strolled idly through an ivy-covered archway. She found herself on a small lawn, surrounded by evergreens. There were several pots and urns of different sizes, but only one sculpture, a pair of lovers crowded together on a rather inadequate pedestal. The young man had a wreath of vine leaves on his head and a drunken smile on his lips. In one hand he held aloft a stone goblet, while on his other arm leaned a young woman, her head on his shoulder, tilted back to smile up into his face.

"Bacchus," Emma said to herself. "The god of wine." She'd never seen him with a girl friend before. She walked closer to them, licking the last of the chocolate off her fingers, when she heard Poppy call.

"Emma! Do come and look at this one! It's a monster!"

With a last careless look at the statue, Emma walked through the arch and was gone.

There was a silence in the little garden. For three minutes nothing moved, not even the leaves on the evergreens. Then the marble girl unwound her arm from the neck of Bacchus and stepped stiffly down from the pedestal onto the grass. Belladonna. Bending down, she picked up some lengths of chain from under the hedge where it had been hidden in the long grass.

A low humming came from her, and as if in answer, a large stone angel stepped out from behind an evergreen. Together they looked at

Bacchus, who now stood alone on his pedestal, smirking foolishly at the sky. Then Belladonna nodded, and moving toward him, bent down . . .

There was the sound of whistling and of something on squeaky wheels being trundled along a flagged path. A young man's voice sang cheerfully.

> "*I wheeled my wheelbarrow*
> *Through paths broad and narrow.*
> *Singing . . .*"

The angel picked up an urn and, holding it on one shoulder, pressed back against an evergreen, working her wings into the branches until they were invisible to all but the keenest eyes. Belladonna hesitated and then stood still, the hand holding the chain behind her back, the other pointing to the sky. But on Bacchus's ankle, dark as a crack against the white marble, one piece of the chain had already been fastened.

> "*Singing statues, fine statues,*
> *Alive, alive—O*"

caroled Mr. Forster's son, coming around the corner, pushing an empty cart in front of him. As he passed Belladonna, her pointing hand clenched into a fist and her eyes moved horribly in their stone lids to watch him.

He never even noticed her. He walked past the

three statues without giving them a glance. If he had turned his head so much as an inch, Belladonna would have killed him. And Emma, too, had she come closer. Not from hate, but carelessly, as one might crush an insect in case it stung. Belladonna had no knowledge of good or evil; like her namesake, the pretty plant that displays its deadly berries to passing children, she could please or kill with equal unconcern.

The young man's song receded into the distance. Then Poppy's voice came through the arch.

"What about in here?"

"No, there's nothing" came Emma's voice. "I've already looked. Let's go this way."

10

Their quarrel began on the moors. All day Poppy
had been on her best behavior. She felt if she
could store up enough credit, God might be in-
clined to forgive the odd lie or two that was bound
to escape her in time. She had been, she considered, friendly, cheerful, and uncomplaining. Yet
there was no doubt that by five o'clock in the afternoon, she seemed to have gotten on Emma's
nerves.

They had been glad to leave Forster's after
lunch; surrounded by its high stone walls, it had
grown hotter and hotter, as if it were an oven
unsuccessfully trying to bake the statues brown.

"There'll be a breeze up on the moors," Emma
had promised. "There's always some wind up there,
even on the hottest day. I love the moors in
summer. It's like heaven."

But the breeze seemed to Poppy no more than
a warm breath in her face. She looked unenthus-

iastically at the sun-baked hills that spread around great gray crags like a petrified sea and thought privately that if this was heaven, then she might as well be a liar and go to hell. She did not say so, however. She was tactful and said nothing.

Poppy had reached the stage in her search when she no longer expected to find Belladonna but went on looking nonetheless. To give up now, before she had looked everywhere, however unlikely, would have seemed like a betrayal. Emma, she knew, only half believed her, but that half was important to Poppy. She did not want to lose it.

If only Emma weren't so bossy, she thought, balancing with one toe on the ground (her bicycle was a little too big for her) and watching her new friend. Emma was so busy, so needlessly efficient, so fond of taking charge. Look at her now, wasting time once again taking a compass reading.

"We're not going to the North Pole, are we?"

"You may laugh," said Emma (she obviously was not going to). "But you can't be too careful on the moors. It's not like London—there aren't any policemen you can ask. People often get lost. Every year. A mist suddenly comes down and they can't find their way back and they die of exposure."

"In summer?"

"The weather can always change," Emma said shortly.

"Come on, Emma. We haven't got all day."

Unfortunately this gave Emma a chance to say it would have been better if Poppy had realized this sooner, instead of haring off down the wrong path just because it was like a switchback and fun to ride over. They must have come miles out of their way!

"Sorry," mumbled Poppy.

"You could've broken your neck! Or the bicycle!" Emma made this sound definitely the worse possibility. "Footpaths are meant for feet, not wheels. It was a mad idea to bring our bikes up here."

"Sorry," Poppy mumbled again. It had, of course, been her idea. "Still," she added hopefully, "we wouldn't have been able to come nearly such a long way without them."

"Since we've been going the wrong way, thanks to you, that might've been a good thing," Emma said sharply.

Poppy looked down guiltily. They had planned, or rather, *Emma* had planned—to cut across to the east, in order to arrive on the moors above Boverley. Belladonna, Emma had decided, had probably missed Forster's altogether. If she had been in Boverley churchyard with the angel last night, she could have gone straight up to the moors from there. Poppy had agreed, though privately she thought the statue might be anywhere. Still, she should have let Emma lead the way.

"Where now?" she asked meekly.

For a moment Emma did not answer. Then she mounted her bicycle and began tolling up a steep hill.

"This way," she called over her shoulder.

Poppy followed. Her legs were beginning to ache, and halfway up the hillside she had to dismount and push her bike. It was almost as if Emma were choosing the steepest hills and the stoniest paths to punish Poppy. If so, she was suffering as much, if not more, herself. Her face was crimson and her breath came in short gasps, like a distressed steam engine. But still she went on.

If she can bear it, so can I, thought Poppy, biting her lip to stop any complaints leaking out. Doggedly she followed Emma up and down until her head spun and the path they were on, which had been getting narrower and narrower, finally petered out altogether. There was only rough grass and rocks.

Emma sat on her bicycle, her feet on the ground, and looked down at where the path should have been. She said nothing. Poppy, after one look at her face, thought she had better keep quiet. She gazed around. The sky was now patterned with dark clouds whose shadows moved like huge black sheep over the golden moors. The sun, appearing and disappearing, now edged a cloud with brightness, now sent down spreading rays to lie upon the side of a hill. Near at hand, among the rocks, a few hyacinths shook gently in the strengthening breeze.

"It *is* quite pretty, isn't it?" Poppy said innocently.

"You bleeding idiot!" shouted Emma. "Can't you understand? We're lost, damn you! We're lost!"

Her voice went ringing out over the hills and died away. An echo answered faintly. Two birds, high above them, called to each other and then were gone. There was silence, except for the tiny noises the wind made playing in the grass and around the rocks.

After a long pause, in which Poppy rejected all the remarks that first came into her mind, she said calmly, "You've got your compass. It's lucky you brought it. If we go due south, we must come off the moors sooner or later, mustn't we? It doesn't matter if it's not at the same place. Once we reach a road, there'll be signposts."

Emma pointed. "That's due south."

It did not look inviting. The rough ground rose sharply. Its threadbare grass, pierced here and there with jagged rock, was strewn all over with loose stones and boulders. This unencouraging sight was crowned with a vast crag, leaning out toward them, against which lumps of stone, as large as houses, were precariously balanced.

"We could go around it," Poppy suggested.

"How long d'you think it'd take?" Emma demanded shrilly. "I'm tired! I want my supper!"

"It's no wonder you're so fat if all you can ever think about is food!" snapped Poppy. She wished she could catch the words back and stuff them in her mouth, but it was too late.

"I hate you!" Emma cried, tears streaming down her face. "I hate you, Poppy Brown! You're horrid! No wonder nobody likes you! I don't want to be your friend anymore! You—you don't know what friendship is!"

She jerked her front wheel around and started pedaling away furiously.

"Fatso!" Poppy shouted after her. "Fatso Podge!"

"Find your own bleeding way back," Emma yelled, looking back over her shoulder. "I hope you fall down a pothole and die!"

With that parting shot, she looked forward again—but too late!

Her front wheel hit a large stone, swerved violently, and hit a rock. Emma flew over the handlebars, over the rock, and disappeared from sight. The bicycle lay on its side, the front wheel buckled, the back wheel still spinning.

"I hope you're dead!" Poppy shouted, and burst into tears.

There was no answer.

11

Emma was lying on the ground on the other side of the rock, her face turned down toward the grass. The dress on her shoulder was torn and bloody, but she was not dead.

Poppy said, "You're not really hurt badly? You're just pretending, aren't you?"

Emma did not answer. Poppy realized she was biting her fingers and trying not to cry.

She knelt down beside her and asked, "Where does it hurt?"

Emma mumbled through her fingers so that it was difficult to hear, but Poppy thought she said, "Everywhere."

Gently Poppy pulled back the torn dress and examined her shoulder. It looked torn, too, and blood was oozing out of it. She must have hit a rock with her shoulder. She was lucky it hadn't been her head.

"It's not too bad," Poppy said hopefully. "Only a graze. No bones poking out."

"My ankle," Emma said indistinctly, pointing.

"Your ankle?" repeated Poppy, wondering how Emma could be hurt at both ends. She must have bounced. "Let's have a look—"

Emma cried out sharply. "Don't touch it!"

"What shall I do, then?"

Immediately Emma shut her eyes. It was like someone pulling down the blind in a shop window just as you were looking in, to show it was no good asking for anything. Emma was injured. It was not up to her anymore to make the decisions. Someone must look after her. She lay on the ground, her fingers in her mouth, looking years younger, like a small child going to sleep in a safe bed.

But your Mommy and Daddy aren't here, thought Poppy. They won't be coming. They don't know where you are. There's *no one* to depend on. There's only me and *I* don't know what to do!

"Wake up, Emma," she said anxiously. "You didn't hit your head! You can't have a concussion *here*!"

Emma gave no sign of having heard her.

"Does your head hurt?"

"My ankle," Emma repeated faintly, without opening her eyes.

Poppy looked at it. Pink and very fat, bulging around the straps of the sandal. Wasn't that how Emma's ankles usually looked? The other foot was out of sight. She decided she had better remove the sandal.

"No!" cried Emma. She turned out to be well enough to make a great deal of fuss, fending off Poppy's hands and whimpering, "Don't! It hurts! Don't!" until Poppy lost her temper and said sharply, "It'll hurt a damn sight more if I don't! You'll get gangrene or something and I'll have to cut your foot off with my little penknife! You are a baby, Emma!"

"I'm not! Daddy says I'm very brave!"

"Then *be* brave!"

They glared at each other. Then Emma turned her head away and bit her lower lip, making no further sound as Poppy struggled with the stiff buckle. The ankle looked enormous and the foot was crisscrossed with indentations where the straps had been. It ought to be bandaged, but of course they didn't have a bandage.

"It doesn't matter," said Emma. "It feels better already."

"Can you put any weight on it?"

"No."

"Not even if I help you?"

"No."

Poppy sighed. It was getting darker. The sun had gone behind a cloud, and the cloud was spreading like an inkstain to cover the whole sky. She saw lightning flicker brilliantly on her left and heard shortly the distant roll of thunder. If the storm came this way, they were going to get very wet. Just behind them, on the steep slope, two tall rocks, meeting at the top, seemed to form a cave, and she helped Emma edge her way over there on her bottom.

"Now you'll keep cozy and dry," she said, pretending not to notice the tears of pain on Emma's cheeks. "While I go—"

"Go? Go where! You can't leave me!"

"Got to get help, old honey, now haven't I? Give me the compass—"

But Emma, seeming to recover all her old strength of mind, was dead against this.

"Only a monster could walk off and leave me alone," she said. "And what makes you think you could find your way back? You're a newcomer, a town girl. From the *South,* too!"

She recounted five fatal accidents that had occurred from townsfolk falling down potholes, seven broken legs, three collarbones; and one Londoner who had gone quite mad and howled like a wolf.

"Do you want to end up like that?" she demanded.

"No," Poppy said meekly, happy to be dissuaded from blundering about the moors on her own in the coming storm. Privately she thought it had been very brave of her to have volunteered; she hoped God had noticed. Now, if honor was satisfied, so was she. As Emma pointed out, they had told enough people where they were going—all they had to do now was wait for the search party.

"They'll see our bicycles," Emma said when Poppy wondered if they ought to move back into the open where they would be visible.

So they made themselves as comfortable as they could, sitting on their sweaters and leaning back against the rock. Watching the forked lightning in the distance, they wondered idly where Belladonna was and what she was doing, and whether she had found any other statues to set free.

"Lucky Forster's lock their gates at night," said Emma. "Never do if that lot got loose. . . ."

For a moment they felt uneasy. They had not looked very carefully, after all. There had been so many little gardens, and it had been so hot. . . . No point worrying now. Like people living on the slopes of a volcano, they found it easy to turn their backs on it. It seemed more important to worry about how much cake Poppy had left and how best to ration the half bottle of orange soda that was all Emma had, and whether Poppy should try to find wood so they could light a fire, if it grew cold. Bit risky in this dry weather, Emma thought. Better not unless they had to. How long would they have to wait?

"Eight o'clock. I said I'd be back by six. They'll be beginning to worry now," Emma said with a trace of satisfaction. "Mommy will keep looking at the clock and out of the window. Then she'll ring up your mother—"

"And Mother Brown will say I'm a wicked girl,

who's not to be trusted, and good riddance to bad rubbish," said Poppy. She had meant to say it lightly, a joke merely, but it came out sounding bitter.

Emma said quickly, the kindness showing, "Don't be silly. Your mother's very fond of you."

"Yes. Sure."

"She is! She loves you. Anyone can see that."

"I know." Poppy did not want to talk about mothers. And she didn't need Emma's pity either. Emma with her Daddy and Mommy, and her big brother, Mike, not to mention her dog and her cat and her hamster and her damn goldfish! Who'd want to live in such a crowd? Poppy was all right on her own, thank you very much!

"Where's that search party got to?" she asked.

"Give them time. Mommy'll be crying soon and telling Daddy to ring the police, but he'll be afraid of making a fool of himself. He'll probably drive up to Forster's and then across to Boverley to see if he can find us."

"And when he doesn't?"

"Then he'll go to the police. Only it's getting dark early tonight. . . ."

"I should've lit that fire. It'd show for miles," said Poppy, getting up and looking out across the moors. The storm seemed to be over. The sky was clearer now and a pale moon had risen, even though the daylight was not yet all gone. A cool, fitful wind had sprung up, whipping at a clump of bent trees and rattling their crooked branches. A small bush shuddered suddenly as if it had come alive.

"There's someone coming!"

There was the sound of running footsteps and a small figure, crouched low and moving fast, came up the slope toward them. It would have gone by without noticing them if Poppy had not stepped out into its path. It shrieked and tried to swerve past her, but she grabbed its arm.

"Leggo! T'angel'll get me!"

It was a boy. He tried to wrench his thin arm out of her grasp but she was too strong for him. He kicked her painfully on the shin.

"Stop that!" she exclaimed, giving him a shake. "Don't be silly, I'm not going to hurt you. You— what angel?"

"Back there," he said, looking fearfully over his shoulder and pointing. "She's after me, she is, but Ah din do nowt! Tha tell 'un Ah din do nowt. Tell 'un . . . Ah'll poot it back!"

"Someone's got a guilty conscience," said Emma, but she sounded uneasy. "Is there really . . . Can you see anyone? Anything?"

"No," said Poppy, straining her eyes, "but it must've been the same one."

"I couldn't run away," said Emma, sounding very frightened, "not with my bad ankle, I mean."

Poppy looked very carefully. "I can't see anything," she said finally. "He must've shaken them off."

She turned to examine her captive. He was a thin, foxy child of about nine, with hair that in full daylight would probably be red but now looked a rusty brown. His complexion was a mixture of dirt, freckles, and spots, with a few clean paths where his tears had run. His nose needed wiping, which he now attended to, with the back of his free hand.

"Tha's hurting me arm," he whined. "Leggo!"

She looked at him suspiciously. "If I let you go, you'll be off like a rabbit—"

"Nao! Ah promise!"

"I can run faster than you," she warned him. "I can catch you any time of the day or night. I'm a very good runner. I—" She was about to claim that she had won gold medals for running but remembered her rash vow just in time. "So if you run away, I'll catch you, and you'll wish I hadn't!"

It was difficult to sound frightening and tell nothing but the truth. Fortunately the boy seemed impressed by the very restraint of her threat and swore on his mother's grave that he wouldn't run away, not till they said he could, cross his heart and hope to die. Poppy released him and he stood, rubbing his arm resentfully.

"What's your name?"

"Rob."

"Do you know where we are?"

"On t'moors, tha daft nit."

"I know that, idiot. What part of the moors? Where's the nearest village?"

He looked around vaguely and then shrugged his thin shoulders.

"Where are you from?"

"Ah's from Boverley."

"Where were you running to?"

"Ah weren't running *to*. Ah was running *from*. Ah's lost. Does tha know where Boverley is, miss?"

When he found they were lost, too, he burst out crying. What with his accent and his voice being thick with tears, Poppy could not understand what he now said, but Emma reported that, unlikely though it might seem, he was a choirboy. He had been chased, he claimed, by the vicar's angel for stealing some candles from St. Peter's. He had *not* taken them. He said he would put them back if he had, but he hadn't. He begged them to save him from the angel. He didn't want to go to hell, nor heaven neither!

"Poor little mite," said Emma.

"I wish he'd blow his nose," said Poppy. "I can't—" She stopped. What was that noise? Not thunder. It was too low. It seemed to come from the very ground itself. . . . Then she saw them.

Figures, some pale, some patched with dark, were moving across the shadowed moors. They came slowly, a crowd of them, and the earth shook beneath their feet. In the fading light she saw a white angel, a naked boy riding a goat, a huge Neptune carrying a trident, a pale queen . . . There were men, women, and children—and creatures she could not name. The leader—it was Bella-donna—walked between two white lions.

The children crouched back in the shadow of their rocks and watched. Poppy could feel Rob shaking against her and hear his teeth chattering.

"Quiet!" she breathed, for the strange procession was now passing them by. The strain of waiting was too much for the boy. He screamed and screamed, trying to scrabble up the rock behind them as if attempting to force his way through.

The statues halted and turned. There was a loud, low humming, and then they started walking toward the terrified children.

12

It was not possible to run away. The boy, seeming to have lost his wits, still scrabbled helplessly at the solid rock behind them. Even if Poppy's legs had not been weak with fright, how could she have left him and Emma? But she could not help remembering, as they were dragged from their cave, the warning proverb—Never catch at a falling knife or a falling friend.

The statues stood around them in a circle, like Stonehenge, and stared at them. Poppy's heart beat like a drum. The boy was still screaming, but his screams had a fading, defeated sound, as if he knew his end had come. The angel was holding him at arm's length, and every now and then, when he stopped for breath, she would shake him as if to see what would happen. When he had screamed himself hoarse and could no longer respond to this treatment, she raised her stone fist and looked toward Belladonna as if for permission.

"No!" shouted Poppy, finding her voice at last. "Don't hurt him! Stop her, Belladonna! Please!"

Belladonna glanced toward Poppy but made no sign. It was a youth, a shepherd boy of extraordinary beauty, who stepped forward to hold back the angel's arm with his crook. Then, putting down both the crook and the lamb he had been carrying, he took the boy by the hair and looked down into his face. Rob, quiet at last, stared back in terror. Gently the shepherd boy put out his stone finger and, catching a tear as it fell from Rob's lashes, carried it over to Belladonna. They studied it curiously as it gleamed faintly in the moonlight.

Poppy, watching now, heard a loud, low humming sound all around her. Something hard poked her in the back. She jumped in fright and found a small group of statues had come up close and were examining her with their pale eyes. Something about the fixed, sweet smiles, the strange faces, the outstretched arms, was horribly familiar. It was like an old nightmare suddenly come to life. . . .

Their stiff fingers poked and pried, caught at her shirt, and raked through her hair. One statue, pulling some strands out by the roots, held its hand up in the moonlight, the fine shining hairs, caught in its stiff fingers, stirring slightly in the wind. It seemed bemused by something so delicate and soft, and fingered its own grim, immobile curls as if dissatisfied.

More hands stretched out toward Poppy's head, as if desiring a share of this strange, soft stuff that grew on it. With a yelp of terror, she dodged and ran blindly into the center of the circle.

"Emma! Rob! Where are you?" she screamed, for she could no longer see them. There were statues everywhere, with their strange blank faces. Then at last she saw Belladonna. Belladonna, her friend, whom she had set free and who surely must love her for it. She ran to her and caught her arm.

"Belladonna, please, oh, please! It's me! Poppy!"

There was no sign of recognition in the face that turned to her.

"Don't you remember me?" said Poppy, trembling. "We were friends! Remember the little garden? How I gave you my bracelet? It was *me* who gave it to you, the chain . . ."

No sign of gratitude in the marble face.

"But we were *friends*! You can't have forgotten! Say something, Belladonna! Say you remember me! You must understand me! You must!"

Belladonna made a low, harsh, muttering sound and waited, watching Poppy, almost as if expecting an answer. In the hollow center of her eyes there was nothing. No kindness, no anger, no malice, just nothing!

"Oh, please!" said Poppy, crying. "You must understand me! *Please!*"

Above the continuous, murmuring hum there suddenly came an odd, loud hooting. Belladonna made a sharp, short sound like a command, and some statues moved back to reveal Emma sitting on the ground. Her dark hair was all pulled about, and her cheeks were wet with tears. One hand was nursing her ankle, while the other was pressed against her mouth trying to muffle her moaning. The rough handling had hurt her body; the sight of moving statues offended her mind. It made nonsense of everything she had ever learned.

"I don't believe it! I don't, no, I don't!" she cried through her fingers. "I want to wake up! Oh, God, I want to wake up!"

Belladonna made a sharp sound and gestured violently with her hand. Up! Up! she seemed to be saying, as if furious that anyone should sit in her presence.

"She can't get up. She's hurt her ankle," Poppy said quickly, coming to Emma's side, pointing to the ankle and miming with her hands as if she were wringing out a dishcloth. "Twisted."

No comprehension in the watching faces.

"Sort of . . . broken," Poppy said helplessly. She made a sharp gesture as if she were snapping a twig.

Belladonna stared. Then, to Poppy's utter horror, appeared to misunderstand. Beckoning the angel, she made a horribly expressive gesture with her hands, of something being crushed, crumpled up like paper, and thrown away.

Immediately the angel started to advance upon Emma. Emma started to shriek, and Poppy, dancing about in terror between Emma and the angel, shouted, "No! Go away! No!"

All the statues stood watching, humming in a high-pitched irregular fashion that sounded horribly like laughter. The angel, playing up to them, did not simply knock Poppy out of her path, but made a game of it, stepping first this way and that, so that Poppy nearly fell over her own feet.

Then the angel leaned forward. Poppy found herself seized by hands so hard that they seemed to grind her very bones, and she half expected to see herself powdering away like flour. The earth fell away and she was up in the sky, held aloft like a baby by white columns of arms, while she kicked and tried in vain to reach with her fist the huge, grinning, upside-down face. Now this vanished from her sight as she was tossed up in the air. She saw the moon spin around the sky like a golden ball. She saw the circle of statues below like an open mouth. . . . The ground rushed up and hit her, knocking all the breath out of her body.

The statues seemed to find this very funny.

"Beast! Bleeding cow!" yelled Poppy, too angry to care what she said. "How could you let her, Belladonna? How could you?" Then, remembering the words Emma had used to her, she added, "You don't know what friendship is!"

To her surprise, for she had given up hope, this remark seemed to go home. Or perhaps it was only the anger and bitterness in her voice that somehow reached the statue. Belladonna's smile slowly faded and she stared at Poppy with a puzzled frown.

Then she beckoned to the angel and the shepherd youth, and they stood humming together. From the way they kept glancing at the children, it was obvious they were discussing them. The other statues had moved back again into their circle, only this time it was smaller. There were no gaps.

Poppy felt her hand tugged and looked down. Rob's dirty, tearstained face, now bleeding from a graze on one cheek, looked up at her.

"Take me 'ome," he whined. "Please, miss." She squeezed his hand helplessly.

Now Belladonna and her two companions began slowly walking around the circle, stopping to talk to the other statues (for their humming could only be some sort of speech) and turning often to glance or gesture toward the children.

They're deciding what to do with us, thought Poppy. They're asking everyone's opinion.

She looked anxiously at Emma and Rob. How scruffy they looked, how dirty and plain. As she must herself. What would they look like to these tall, unchanging, perfect beings, so beautiful in the moonlight? Rubbish, no doubt. Flimsy, ill-made . . . expendable.

"Don't sniff! Haven't you got a hanky?" she whispered angrily to Rob. "Stand up straight, can't you!"

For he was crouched like a runner at the start of a race, and his eyes looked this way and that for the chance to make a bolt for it.

"You'd never do it!" she hissed. "Do you want to get us all killed!"

Belladonna and her companions had reached the huge Father Neptune, and as Poppy watched, he made a downward stabbing movement with his trident. It was impossible to mistake his meaning. There was one vote against them. And from the appreciative hum that followed, many were in agreement.

"Can't you think of anything?" Poppy whispered fiercely to Emma. "You're supposed to be clever! Go on! Be clever!"

Poor Emma stared back blankly. She was clutching her knapsack, which she must have been holding when they were dragged out of the cave. Now, while she still stared in front of her, one of her hands moved sideways like a crab, disappeared into the knapsack, and came out holding a box of matches. She did not say anything but just sat there, holding them.

Poppy squatted down in front of her, pretending to be examining her ankle.

"What's that for?" she whispered.

Emma did not answer. She seemed to have lost her voice.

"They won't be afraid of fire," Poppy whispered, disappointed. "Stones don't burn."

She stood up in time to see another statue clench his fist and bring it down sharply, as if hammering something. And another, and another. . . . Why? What had they done? How had they offended the statues? Just by being different?

She looked desperately around the smiling faces. They weren't even angry. She could hear their high-pitched humming laughter. Were they really going to kill them, just for an evening's entertainment? Or from curiosity, like a small child taking a clock apart to see how it worked? Didn't they know it was wrong to hurt people? Didn't they even know about pain? She *must* make them understand!

She ran forward, crying, "Please! What are you going to do? Don't hurt us! We haven't done anything! Belladonna—"

Belladonna looked at her and turned away. Poppy glanced at the shepherd boy, and it seemed that he looked at her kindly. She caught hold of his arm.

"We can help you. We're not worthless, honest!" she said, pleading. "We can tell you things. You're new to it all, there'll be lots you don't know. We can help. . . ."

Slowly he moved a hand up toward her face. So gentle was his smile, so warm, that she thought he was going to stroke her cheek and did not move away. Instead his cold fingers gripped her by the chin and he forced her mouth open. She started to struggle, but it was so painful that she stopped. She thought he was going to break her jaw. She stood still while he gazed curiously into her mouth. Then, still smiling, he let her go and turned away.

"We can't help you if you kill us!" Poppy shouted. "Because we'd be dead and then it'll be too late! Ask her." She pointed to the angel. "She must know about death! She stood in Boverley churchyard long enough—ask her if they talk at night!"

The statues hummed. They looked curiously at Poppy's pointing finger. Looked at their own fingers. Began pointing with them, first at random, then suddenly seeming to get the idea, they all turned and pointed at the angel.

The angel, made uneasy by all this attention and knowing where to put the blame, advanced furiously on Poppy. . . .

Emma struck a match. She held it to the little pile of torn paper and dry grass she had made, unnoticed, while Poppy was talking. The flame wobbled wildly in the wind. Then the paper flared up, caught the dry grass on which it was lying, and little flames ran before the wind across the grass, while the statues parted in surprise to make way for it. A small brush began to burn brightly on the far side of the circle, while the statues, like children with a new toy, crowded in to look at it.

"Run!" said Emma. "Go on, run for it!"

Rob was off like a hare and vanished into the night.

Poppy hesitated, taken by surprise.

"Run, damn you, run!" said Emma, crying.

Poppy ran.

She ran for about ten yards and then tripped and fell onto her knees. She looked back. The statues were still milling about in the smoky moonlight, but the flames were dying down. Emma was inching her way over the rough ground. She had traveled about three feet on her bottom and was obviously not going to make it. Already some of the statues were turning.

Poppy got to her feet and hesitated, trembling. She wanted to run and run, to get away, to be safe again! What good could she do by going back? They would *both* be killed! Why should she give up her life for Emma? She didn't need friends! She'd done without them before! Run, Poppy, run! she told herself, but her feet would not move.

She saw the angel lurch away from the smoke. She saw it look around and catch sight of Emma. She heard Emma sob.

A multitude of thoughts and memories tumbled through her mind—her room at Charle, clean, neat, with all her belongings in rows that nobody disturbed or borrowed or broke; the small garden where she used to sit alone, talking to a statue that never answered; Emma in the cellar, with her tumbled hair and dirty face, looking hurt. Emma sitting by the goldfish pond at Forster's, sharing her chocolate, and laughing, bumping over the moors together on their bicycles. . . .

She blinked. She saw the advancing angel, beautiful, implacable, and cold. She saw Emma, soft, quivering, dirty, weeping in terror. . . .

She ran back to Emma's side.

13

Rob, crouching in a clump of low bushes and trying to swallow the whole night into his heaving
lungs, heard a man's voice in the distance.

"Emma! Emma! Emma!" it called.

"Ah'm here! Ah can tell tha where she is! Wait
for me!" Rob wanted to say, but he had too little
breath to spare. All that came out was a squeak so
high and small that only a passing owl heard it.

"Ah'm here! Ah'm here!" cried Rob, limping as
fast as he could to where the voice had come out
of the night.

It came again, more faintly, as if the unseen
caller were retreating even as Rob advanced.

"Emma! Emma!" and then, "Poppy!"

Please hear me, please wait for me. There's
monsters about tonight, please save me! thought
Rob, but all his tired voice could manage was
one more hoarse "Here!" which the wind took hold
of and tossed carelessly away.

There was the distant sound of a car door

slamming; the sound of an engine starting up—and fading into the night. Rob burst into tears. Then, wiping them away, he hobbled painfully to where he now knew the road must be.

The strange procession was on the move again, striding across the moors. In the middle, Poppy walked with her head down, hardly knowing what she was doing, so tired that every now and then her eyelids shut without her noticing it, and she would walk blindly on, left, right, left, right . . . Then she would stumble, only to be thrust forward again by a hard hand.

Left, right, left . . . Should've left when you had the chance. Now you've gone down with your falling friend, Poppy, my girl, she told herself, right to the bottom. Rock bottom. Rock—stone—statue . . . There was a joke somewhere there, she thought sleepily. She must share it with Emma. . . .

But in front of her Emma, being carried over Neptune's shoulder because she could not walk, had her eyes shut and looked as if she would never see a joke again. Her face, pale and ghastly in the moonlight, wobbled helplessly like a tied balloon.

"Emma! Emma, are you all right?"

To Poppy's great relief, Emma opened her eyes.

"Not—too—bad," she said, the words being bumped out of her.

"Does your ankle still hurt?"

"Not—very—much."

Brave, untruthful Emma. Poppy decided not to tell her about the ache in her own knees and the blisters on both her heels. If only they could rest.

She looked from under her lashes at the tall white figure striding beside her. Her jailer. He was supposed to be a god of some sort, Emma had said earlier. The god of birds, perhaps? He was wearing wings on his hat and at his ankles. He walked rather like a bird, too. A stiff-legged strut, like a seagull, sharp-nosed and jerky. What had Emma called him? Mercury, that was it. Like in thermometers. She remembered because it seemed an odd name for a god.

"Please—Mr. Mercury, sir."

His eyes moved but he did not answer. His hand, she knew, was hard. Could he be moved by tears?

"Please, can we stop for a rest? Please, sir?"

He ignored her. Perhaps he had not understood.

"I'm so tired," she said, sniffing. "My feet hurt. My heels are rubbed to rags. Look—" She hopped on one foot, trying to show him the blister on the other.

The only response she got was another hard push in the back that sent her staggering forward, so that she stubbed her toe on a loose stone and nearly fell flat on her face. Tears filled her eyes, and she looked down to hide them, in case Emma was watching.

On and on they marched, into the night.

"*Left—left*—you *had* a good home and you *left* it."

The old marching jingle came into her mind. One of her foster parents, Ex-Sergeant-Major Allen, had taught it to her. Putting his arm through hers, he used to march her to school through the cold winter streets, chanting under his breath, "*Left—left*—you *had* a good home and you *left* it."

He thought she cried because she didn't want to go to school. He never realized it was because she found the jingle so sad. All those young soldiers, marching away from their good homes. How many good homes had she left? Good-bye, Foster-Mother Allen, good-bye, House-Mother Radlett. So many mothers, always calling her m'dear and my pet. Why? Because they couldn't remember her name.

Pansy? they would say hopefully. Rose? Lily, Flora, Ivy? They knew it was the name of a flower, but which one? She never stayed long enough for them to be certain. Easier just to say m'dear and be done with it.

Rot 'em all! she thought fiercely, I don't care! People, statues, it's all the same to me. I'll be all right . . . right . . . right . . .

The procession stopped so suddenly that she crashed into Neptune, banging herself painfully on his hard elbow and waking Emma.

"What is it? What's happened?" Emma cried.

"I don't know."

"They've stopped."

"Yes."

"Why?"

Poppy stood on tiptoe, but Neptune was too broad and too tall. She tried to step out far enough to see the head of the column but was jerked roughly back into line by her keeper.

"I can't see," she said.

Emma turned her head, but she was hanging too far over Neptune's shoulder and could only see a little sky, half a moon, and a great expanse of marble.

"It's no good. I can't either."

"We'll just have to wait," said Poppy, glad not to be walking anymore.

They waited.

Time passed. The statues waited patiently. In silence. They stood so still that by comparison the moon seemed to be racing across the sky. Emma had fallen asleep and was snoring quietly.

Another five minutes. And another.

Poppy shifted from one foot to the other and back again. She scratched her head, her arm, her back. She wriggled her shoulders. She sighed.

They were good at waiting. After all, they were statues, she thought. I shall grow old waiting, she thought. My hair will turn gray, then white, then fall out—but *they* won't change.

How very still they were. Perhaps whatever power the lightning had given them had run out and they would never move again.

"Mr. Mercury, sir—" she said cautiously.

He turned his head. Little cracks ran over his neck and cheeks, just as they had at first with Belladonna. She stared at him. You've stood so still, you've gone stiff, she thought, but she did not say it aloud.

Someone was standing on the other side of her.

She turned sharply and saw it was the shepherd boy. He, too, was looking at the cracks, now fading, on Mercury's cheeks, and his expression was thoughtful. Then, seeing her look at him, he smiled his warm, gentle smile, which seemed to hold so much sweetness, and pointed forward with one hand.

The procession had started moving forward without her noticing it while she had been standing watching Mercury. Neptune, still carrying Emma, was some yards ahead. She had time to see, as she hurried to catch up before anyone should think it necessary to push her, that the figures in front appeared to be vanishing into the side of the hill itself.

It's the hole, she thought in terror, remembering the gardener's warning. No one will find us now.

14

Rob limped wearily into Boverley. No one was around. The houses were in darkness; only here and there a light showed in a bedroom window. The Red Lion, its paint looking black in the moonlight, creaked in the night wind. The pub was closed; his father would be at home.

Keeping to the shadows and looking frequently over his shoulder, Rob turned into Bacon Lane and came at last to a small, damp stone cottage, where everything that was not made of stone was broken or apt to crumble at a touch. Home, he thought with satisfaction.

He hobbled up the cracked concrete path that led around the side of the house. The kitchen light was on, shining out to welcome him, and the door had been left unlocked. As he entered, old Prince looked up from his box on the floor, peering at Rob with his dim, milky eyes, and thumped his tail twice in greeting before going back to sleep. Rob turned the key in the lock and then forced the old rusty bolt across.

Safe. No one could get at him now. He was home.

Except for the old dog, the kitchen was uninhabited. A dozen or so empty beer bottles and some crumpled potato chip bags were on the table, and the chipped saucer that did duty as an ashtray was overflowing with cigarette ends and the chewed butt of a cigar. The Boverley Darts' Team had been celebrating long past closing time. But where was their champion?

Rob went into the front parlor and switched on the light. There, asleep on the couch, rosy and snoring, was his father.

Some kind friend had loosened his collar and taken off his shoes. Another had fetched a blanket from upstairs and laid it over him. Some thoughtful hand had placed a plastic bowl on the floor by his side. The only thing they hadn't been able to do was get him up the steep, narrow stairs to his bed. He was a big man.

Rob stood for a moment, looking down at him. He shrugged. Then he looked across to the uncurtained window where the night showed black.

It's nowt to do with me, he thought. Not my friends. Never seen 'em before. But the one called Poppy, he remembered, had said, "Don't hurt him!" and the fat one had said, "Run!"

He turned back to his father, and leaning down,

shouted onto a large red ear. "Dad! Wake up then! Wake up!"

His father stirred beneath the blanket and belched.

"Dad! There's summat bad going on up t'moors. Tha's got t'wake!"

"Whazzat?"

"Ah'm telling ya. There's two girls—"

"Go 'way!"

"One's 'urt—"

His father groaned. "Tha'll be 'urt, lad, if tha don't scram," he mumbled.

"Dad, listen! T'monsters got 'em."

One bloodshot eye opened and regarded him pathetically. "Tha's bin dreaming. Go 'way, there's a good lad, or I'll belt ya one. Go back t'bed. Can't tha see tha father's sick?"

"Tha's not sick, tha's drunk!" Rob said bitterly. "That's what ails ya. The drink's got ya and tha'll be daft till morning."

He left his father snoring and went up to his own room. He did not put on the light. Opening his window wide, he leaned out and looked searchingly into the tangled garden below.

What was that moving?

A black cat hurried across the silver grass, intent on its own business. Trees tossed in the wind, their branches snatching at the moon. A single gray towel flapped on the clothesline.

What was that!

Rob leaped into bed and pulled the blanket over his head.

"O Lord," he prayed, "call off tha bleeding angel!"

As soon as Poppy saw the gaping black hole into which the procession was disappearing, her feet stopped of their own accord, but it was no good. Hard hands grabbed her from behind and swung her off her feet. She had a last glimpse of the shepherd boy's smiling face, and the moonlit moors behind it; then she was in the dark.

At first she could see nothing. She was roughly dumped down against something hard and something soft. The something soft immediately began to whimper. Its ankle hurt. Its bed was cold. Why was it so dark?

"Put on the light," demanded Emma, waking from a dream of home.

"Emma, it's me," whispered Poppy.

There was a short silence as Emma came fully awake. Then she said, "Oh, God, no! Please, no! I can't—I don't—" and began to shudder.

Her shudders shook Poppy, and there was an odd little noise. Someone's teeth were chattering. It might be Emma's. It might be her own. Poppy huddled against the hard rock and the soft shaking Emma and tried to make herself as small as possible. Thunderous feet passed and repassed in front of them. Her eyes, now accustomed to the gloom, watched in numb amazement the dim, gray figures lumbering by, each carrying in its arms a huge rock. It was like a vision from a cold hell, with the Devil's furnace being cleared of clinkers.

As the figures came to the entrance of this ghastly place, she saw them more clearly, silhouetted against a patch of night sky, and she realized what they were doing. They were blocking up the opening. Already the pile of rocks was waist high. Soon it would be quite closed. They would be shut in the dark forever.

Her mind was dazed. It was as if she had shut out terror for another time, another day, perhaps, when she felt stronger. She could not face it now. Besides, there was something distracting her.

"Emma," she whispered, "I gotta go—"

"Don't leave me—"

"I need to pee. I won't be a sec."

She looked toward the diminishing patch of sky. The statues were standing just inside the entrance, holding their rocks and stones ready. She looked the other way, into a darkness her eyes could not penetrate but from which there seemed to come a faint, damp breath of air. She stretched out her hand and her fingers met nothing. She got carefully to her feet.

"Where are you going?" Emma asked tearfully.

"I told you."

"Don't go!"

"D'you want me to wet my pants?" Poppy asked crossly.

She was suddenly furious with Emma, though she knew it was unfair. Emma had given her a chance to run for it, and it was her own fault that she hadn't taken it. But why did she have to strain her stupid fat ankle in the first place?

She slid her left foot forward, then her right, keeping one hand on the rock wall beside her and one stretched out in front of her. She had taken three steps forward in this way when the ground vanished. Her foot waved wildly in empty air. She threw herself backward, hard onto hard rock, bump, bump, bump down three steps, before she managed to stop.

She must have cried out because Emma called anxiously, "What's happened? Poppy? *Poppy?*"

"Nothing."

A flight of steps! She felt the edge of the one she was sitting on with her fingers, and then the one above. They were too regular, she thought, to be accidental ledges. They were man-made steps, cut out of the solid rock and leading down into the darkness.

"Poppy!" called Emma.

"Just a minute."

It must be an old mine, not a cave. There might be several tunnels. If she went on . . .

"Poppy!" cried Emma, sounding on the verge of hysteria.

"Oh, all *right!*" shouted Poppy, and turned around. . . .

The patch of sky was gone. There was no light left behind her. Something moved in the dark. She could sense it coming nearer. She felt herself lifted up and flung over a stone shoulder.

"Emma!" she cried, stretching out her hand, but her fingers only touched rough stone. Whether it was another statue or the rocky wall of the mine itself, she could not tell.

"Emma!" she screamed, as she was carried down into a darkness more complete, more terrible than she had ever known before. "Emma!"

"Poppy!" came the answer from behind her.

"Poppy!" It came again from in front.

"Poppy! Poppy!" from every side as the echo teased her. "Poppy, where are you?"

She did not know. She could see nothing. No glimmer of light, no slight gradation in the dark. Below her she could hear swishing, watery noises, and the air smelled dank.

She screamed just once more, and then she was silent.

15

Poppy was dreaming she was a small child again, riding on her father's shoulder. Only her father was no longer warm and kind, but cold and did not want her. He gave an enormous shrug, as if to be rid of her, and she would have fallen had not someone caught hold of her and lifted her up.

"Dad!" she cried. "I want my Dad!" but the hands holding her would not let her go. They lifted her higher and higher, and she was afraid and cried to be put down. Her hand touched a face. The face was hard and cold, the open eyes unblinking.

It was the noise that woke her. She opened her eyes and saw nothing. It was pitch black. But now, instead of being carried like a sack, she found herself precariously balanced on a slippery marble shoulder, clinging to an unknown head, while from all around there arose a terrible commotion. The watery sounds were gone. Instead there came a loud, discordant humming and grunting, a banging and crashing, a grinding and scraping that beat on her eardrums like a mad musician. Several times something banged into the statue carrying her with a jolt that nearly shook her from her perch. She held on with all her strength, afraid that if she fell off into all the hubbub below she would be killed. Whatever was going on, it was no place for a creature of flesh and blood.

Fortunately, her bearer seemed to agree. After forcing its way through the noisy and crowded dark, it lifted her up and placed her, like a doll, on a high shelf above its head. Instinctively she drew her feet in, out of harm's way. Just in time. There was another crash just below her. An angry humming. Then something was dumped next to her. She knew it was Emma because she was crying, "My ankle! Oh, my shoulder! Look out! My poor leg!"

"Emma," said Poppy, putting out a hand.

"Poppy!" Emma cried thankfully.

The two children clung together and listened in terror to the strange clamor below them. After a while they moved back from the edge until they came to a rock wall behind them, against which they leaned, exhausted. The crashing and banging diminished. The humming became softer and lower. The children slept.

When Poppy woke up, the first thing she saw was her own hand. She lay for a moment staring at it, wondering why the sight of it should surprise her, for there was nothing wrong with it as far as she could tell. All five fingers were there, very dirty but . . . She sat up. She could *see!* There was light!

Grayish in color, as if it had squandered its brightness elsewhere, the light came from some cracks and small apertures in the rock ceiling far above her head and fell in dim, dusty shafts into the cave below. One of these, falling on the wide ledge on which they had slept, circled the children like a weak spotlight in a pantomime.

Emma was still sleeping. Her mouth was open and her lashes looked spiky, as if they had been wet and were stuck together. Every now and then she twitched and whimpered like a dreaming dog. Poppy hesitated. Should she wake her? Not yet.

From the roof of the cave, a single stalactite hung down, like a pointing finger. Poppy crept forward on her hands and knees and peered over the edge.

They were there, as she had known they would be, for the sound of their humming had been in her ears when she woke. Whatever statue had placed her and Emma on the ledge must have been very tall, because the floor of the cave was a long way down and it was as if she looked into a pit.

In the dim light the statues looked gray and insubstantial. Now appearing, now disappearing, they moved in and out of the shadows, like ghostly prisoners at exercise. Now and again one of the walkers would tap a seated figure on the shoulder and they would change places. No one was allowed to sit still for too long.

It's the cracks, thought Poppy, remembering. They're frightened of getting the cracks.

How awkward they looked! How little at home in their human shape. (For a moment she was moved by an echo of sympathy. Was that how she had appeared in other people's homes—so wrong, so out of place, not belonging?) Was that why she and Emma had been spared? Were the statues hoping to learn from them how to be human, as if they were examples to be followed exactly? But how can we teach them? she puzzled. We *are* human. We do it naturally, without thinking.

She saw Belladonna and the shepherd boy, standing close together in a dusty shaft of light. Silver gray and smiling. Nymph and shepherd, she thought, remembering the words of an old song. They looked like lovers—but what a banging of stone lips if they tried to kiss! They were monsters, for all their beauty. They were made of the wrong material. The moment they moved, they were monsters.

On the right she saw a dark gleam of water, where an underground canal emerged into the cave through a tunnel in the rock so small that Poppy could hardly believe it was the way they must have come through; it looked like a large waste pipe. Sitting by the edge of the water was a small boy carrying a large fish. He kept looking into the mouth of the fish and then down at the water, as if he dimly knew there was some connection between the two.

A small boy riding a goat came up. Poppy recognized him from Forster's. It was Chipnose. The fountain boy was bending down, now trying to dip the nose of his fish into the water, when the goat, who seemed unable to control his legs, knocked into him with a loud crash and nearly toppled him into the canal.

Recovering his balance, the fountain boy promptly hit the goat across its knees with his fish. Goat and rider hummed furiously and would have retaliated, had not Mercury come up behind them, given each child a bang on the head, and sent them on their way.

She moved silently back to Emma and looked around. To her right, the shelf they were on narrowed and finally disappeared into the sheer side of the cave. To the left, it widened, started going uphill, came to a rock step or wall about ten feet high, and then, so far as she could see, continued on this level. The rock at this point was rough and pitted. It was not an easy climb, but possible. For someone with two feet.

She looked down at the sleeping Emma, lying in a patch of light, looking oddly like a sacrifice. Emma with her bad ankle. She sighed.

She put her hand over Emma's mouth. Emma's

eyes flew open, wide with fear. Poppy could feel her lips move under her fingers as if to scream.

"Shhh!" she whispered.

Emma's eyes rolled nervously, but she nodded. Poppy removed her hand.

"Don't make a sound," she whispered. "They're down there. Hear them?"

Emma nodded. Her mouth quivered, and she bit her lower lip to steady it.

"See that ledge? Up there?"

Emma looked at it and then back at Poppy and nodded again.

"If we climb up there, we'd be safe. I don't think they could reach us. They're so heavy. I doubt if they can climb."

Emma looked as if she thought she was so heavy she doubted if she could climb either.

"My ankle . . ." she whispered.

They both looked at it. Poppy tried to persuade herself that the swelling had gone down. Then she remembered one of her house fathers used to go climbing in Wales every year and what he'd told her.

"Handholds are more important than footholds," she whispered, thinking for the first time there were some advantages in being fostered out so often. One collected a good deal of odd information. " 'Your foot might slip, but your hand will grip,' " she quoted softly.

Emma looked unconvinced.

"You've got to make the effort," Poppy said urgently. "They're hitting out down there, Emma. Great stone fists. Off with your head! Come *on*!"

It proved as difficult as Poppy had feared getting Emma up on to the higher ledge. They were cold with fear; they were hot with exertion. Their mouths were dry; their hands slippery with sweat. Clothes were torn and skin grazed, and still Emma was only halfway up, clinging to the rock with two hands and one foot while Poppy reached down from above, her arm ten inches too short.

"Come *on*!"

"I can't!" Emma whispered weakly. "I can't move. You go on, Poppy."

"We've had all this before," Poppy whispered crossly. "You're getting up here if I have to throw you up myself."

"I can't! I've got a cramp in my leg!"

"Rot your leg! Look, there's a good handhold. No, to your left! There! There! Yes!"

Poppy leaned over and managed to grasp Emma's wrist, pulling till she felt her bones crack. For a moment she thought they must both fall, two falling friends with no one to catch them; then with a slither and a flop, like a huge landed fish, Emma was on the ledge beside her. They lay there, getting their breath back and smiling at each other.

Then Poppy sat up and looked over her shoulder. It was darker on this ledge than on the one below. The rays of light missed it completely. She strained her eyes to see where it led, trying to persuade herself that it did lead somewhere and that the solid darkness ahead was merely shadow and not rock.

Emma was looking in her knapsack, which she'd had on her back and which had been very much in the way. Her hand rustled in a remaining paper bag and came away empty.

Poppy stared at the knapsack. Considering it had twice hit her on the head when she'd been trying to push Emma up the rock, she must have known Emma still had it, but only now did she realize . . .

"All last night," she whispered bitterly, "all last night, Emma, you had a flashlight on you!"

Emma did not answer but just looked guilty.

"I suppose the flashlight *is* still in your knapsack?"

Emma nodded. "I thought—I didn't think—"

"You *should* think! Try it some time. You'll find it works wonders."

"I thought they'd take it away. If they knew I had it. I thought if I kept it dark—"

"Dark!"

"—then if we got a chance to escape, it would give us an advantage."

"You were the one with the advantage," said Poppy, her voice rising shrilly. Remembering her terror in the dark, she was suddenly very angry. Too angry to notice the statues had stopped humming. She went on complaining, her voice loud in the silence.

"I'm sorry!" said Emma, dismayed. She grabbed the flashlight out of her knapsack and thrust it at Poppy. "Look, you take it now—"

Now it was light? Oh, thank you very much! Poppy pushed Emma's hand away crossly.

The flashlight slipped from her fingers, bounced once on the ledge . . .

"Catch it!" cried Emma, and they both snatched out with their hands, getting in each other's way, missing.

The girls looked down and the statues looked up, all watching the flashlight fall. It hit the floor of the cave and broke in two. The top rolled across to the feet of the shepherd boy, who picked it up and stared at it curiously.

Belladonna, glaring up at the children, opened her mouth and the whole cave rang with her terrible stone shouting.

16

Poppy looked along the ledge, straining her eyes in an attempt to make them see something different —a door perhaps, marked EXIT in neon light, or at least another tunnel, another ledge. Anything but the dark shadow that was now unmistakably a sheer wall of solid rock, arching up to form the ceiling of the cave. They had, she judged, about nine feet of rock shelf for a home, with no modern conveniences whatsoever.

She looked down. Belladonna was beckoning imperiously.

Come down? Not a chance. Not a hope. You're too rough for us. Go and play by yourselves.

Belladonna stood glaring up at them, with her legs apart and her hands clenched into fists. Poppy suddenly remembered a small boy she had once seen at a nursery school standing in just such a pose, screaming because the toy he wanted was out of reach. When it had been given to him, he had promptly taken it apart, and failing to put it together again, had kicked the bits all over the floor. It was not a comforting memory. She wished she had not thought of it.

More beckoning. Another shout.

"Go and stuff yourself!" she shouted back.

"Don't annoy her," Emma said nervously.

"They can't reach us up here."

"I know. But . . ." Emma too had looked along the ledge and seen that it led nowhere. "We might have to bargain with them later."

Bargain? How, and with what? What could they offer in exchange for food and water? The statues had only to wait for them to die of hunger and thirst.

Poppy shut her eyes. I don't want to die, she thought. Not now! Not here in this horrid cave! Not before my birthday! Please God, I don't want to die.

There was an angry humming, like a wasps' nest disturbed.

Poppy opened her eyes again. She saw fists rise and fall like hammers. Feet stamped on the ground like thunder.

"Are you *sure* they can't reach us?" whispered Emma, pressing back against the rock wall until every knob of her spine was in danger of being flattened.

The statues seemed to be having an argument. Neptune and Mercury confronted Belladonna, their humming discordant and shrill. Belladonna suddenly roared very loudly. Neptune bellowed like a bull and showed her his huge fist without, however, actually hitting her. He and Mercury then left the group, followed by a dozen or so others, and came and stood below Poppy and Emma, looking up at them.

"Go away!" shouted Poppy.

"They can't get us up here," said Emma, "can they? Can they, Poppy?"

Neptune had moved over the lower ledge. He could reach it easily with his hands. It was probably he who had placed them there last night, for most of the other statues were smaller. His stiff fingers grated on the rock as he tried to get a grip. He was too heavy. Try as he might, he was not able to pull himself up.

More statues gathered around him, humming with excitement and seeming, by their gestures, to be offering advice. At last only Belladonna and the shepherd boy stood apart, hand in hand, watching.

"Belladonna!" shouted Poppy. "Stop them! Please!"

Belladonna stared at her. Her smile seemed bewildered, as if for the first time her stone heart was touched by feeling, and she was surprised that it hurt. She did not move.

Now Neptune was trying to lift a smaller statue, not a cherub but a dainty Apollo, no taller than

Poppy. Slim and delicate as he looked, he was heavy. Neptune staggered and had to put him down. Mercury came to help him. Together they hoisted him up but still could not quite place him on the ledge.

"Stop it!" shouted Poppy, looking around in vain for something to throw. "You'll only hurt yourselves! Go away!"

Neptune knelt down. Mercury and Winter placed the small Apollo on his shoulders, from where he stepped neatly up onto the ledge.

"Oh! Oh, Poppy!" cried Emma. "He won't be able to climb up this far, will he?"

"If he tries, push him off!"

The Apollo walked along the lower ledge toward them. It was as well for him that the ledge was wide, as he walked with the stiff, lurching movement they all had and might easily have fallen off. He was directly below them now, reaching up with his hands. He was nowhere near tall enough.

"Go away, Titch! You'll never do it!" yelled Poppy.

His pale, hollowed-out eyes stared up at her for a moment. It was impossible to tell what he was thinking. He was smiling when he turned to study the rough rock wall up which she and Emma had climbed. Poppy hated smilers. She would never, ever smile again. Not even if she got the chance.

"Go away!" she screamed.

He took no notice but instead, grasping the

hand holds, began to climb. He was not very good at it. His stone fingers were too stiff to grip properly. His toes could not separate to cling to the rough rock. It was obvious he would never make it. Poppy began, absurdly, to worry on his behalf.

"Be careful! You'll fall!" she said warningly.

"Let him!" Emma said fiercely.

Halfway up his foot slipped. He clung for a moment by one hand, his other seeking wildly for a hold. There was the sound of stone grating against stone as his fingers began to slip, and he looked up at Poppy, his mouth open in a silent cry for help. She stretched out her hand without thinking, without knowing whether she meant to push him off or, foolishly, try to pull him to safety. Whichever it was, she was too late.

Before her fingers reached his, he fell.

He crashed to the floor of the cave. His head broke off and bounced high in the air. For an awful moment the pale eyes stared reproachfully into Poppy's while from the open mouth came a shrill screaming. Then the head fell down again, bounced twice more, and rolled like a ball until it reached Belladonna, where it lay face upward, still complaining. She picked it up and cradled it in her arms as if it were a crying baby.

"Look! Look!" cried Emma, pointing.

The headless body of Apollo was on its feet, holding its hands out blindly, lurching this way and that, banging noisily into other statues.

"You're dead!" Poppy yelled hysterically. "Lie down! You're dead!"

Two statues held Apollo by his arms and quieted him. They were all silent now, staring at the head in Belladonna's hands. Its whimpering had died away.

Belladonna brought it up to her face and stared into its eyes. She shook it. She tried to place it on Apollo's neck, but some pieces were missing and it would not balance.

A terrible, desolate moaning came from her, like an animal in pain. Then with a wild cry, she threw the head at Poppy. It hit the rock just below her, bounced off, and in falling, knocked the head off a shepherdess.

Immediately there was pandemonium. The statues, enraged, began to attack each other furiously. Neighbor turned on neighbor for no better reason than proximity. Fury filled them like steam in a kettle that had to burst out any way it could. They only knew they were angry, not why or with whom. With a terrible clamor, they knocked off each other's heads, arms, legs. Those who had hands left picked up the fallen limbs and used them for more slaughter. A large stone fish flew through the air and fell into the canal with a tremendous splash.

Bewildered, dazed with fear, Poppy watched them. Why were they killing each other? What possessed them? Why could they feel such anger and hate, but not pity or love? Where could they have learned . . . Not from her! Surely, not from her! She only hated them because she was afraid. . . .

"Look!" Emma cried suddenly.

One statue had remembered them. One statue was ignoring the mighty battle behind him in an attempt to get at them. Neptune's protruding eyes glared as he slipped and stumbled and clawed in his efforts to reach them. The girls moved back as far as they could, watched him, and trembled.

On the far side of the lower ledge, jutting out like a narrow fireplace hood, part of the rock wall leaned inward. There was a large crack, running right up to the roof, on this side of it, into which Neptune was able to put his hand and wedge one of his mighty feet. He clung to this projecting bulge as if he were hugging it, and finding some foothold on the side they could not see, began edging his way up. It was not easy, owing to the forward tilt of the rock, but slowly, an inch at a time, he nudged his way upward.

Then it happened. There was a sharp crack. The rock on which Neptune clung began to tilt. The whole wall of stone began to move, seemed to turn to water, a great gray tidal wave that reared above their heads and descended with a terrible roar.

Poppy tried to burrow into the rock. Huddled against Emma, she hid her head beneath her arms, waiting to be drowned in stone. She expected her past life to flash before her eyes, as she had heard was the custom when one drowned, but this small favor was denied her. She saw nothing, and her ears were deafened. Something hit her sharply on the back. And again. Then it was as if somebody had emptied a bucket of gravel on her head. Still she crouched, unmoving, while the dust settled on the great fallen rocks and on the two children safe on their ledge. There was silence, except for a gentle pattering as the last tiny particle of stone found a resting place.

"I think I've gone deaf," said Poppy. She opened her eyes and sat up.

Sunlight was streaming down like a blessing. Looking up through a great new opening in the roof of the cave, she saw the blue sky.

Beside her, the dusty heap that was Emma began to stir and to sneeze. Poppy looked down.

Where the floor had once been, there was now a vast untidy heap of rocks. Half the cave had fallen in and buried the statues. Stone had returned to stone. Only over there, on a bare patch of rock by the side of the canal, lay the pale hands of a child, holding a small stone flower.

"You're crying!" said Emma, seeing with surprise a tear washing a crooked path down Poppy's dusty cheek. She herself was filling with a slow joy, as warm and gentle as the sunlight on her bruised skin.

"No," said Poppy. "No, I'm not" and then felt

guilty at denying her one tear as a gift for poor Chipnose and the fountain boy and all the other sad, heavy children.

Why had they been destroyed? It had not been their fault. The lightning, disturbing their atoms to strange new patterns, had woken them from their long stone sleep; and finding themselves in human shape, they had tried to be human. And failed.

Poor souls, thought Poppy, and then, with a pang, realized they were only poor. They had no souls. They had never had a chance.

"After all, they weren't even animal," she said sadly. "They were only mineral."

She looked up at the blue sky so far above their heads, so fair—and so inaccessible. Then down to the tumbled rocks and the narrow canal, its dark water scummed with dust, leading to the horrible black tunnel, with the stone steps at the other end and the blocked-up opening to the moors.

"How are we going to get out?" she asked.

17

It seemed that every sharp-eyed, shrill-voiced, jumping boy in Boverley had seen two girls last night: on foot or on bikes, on ponies or in cars, all going off in every possible direction. The large policeman was patient. It was his job to listen. But there are limits—and the very limit in this case was a small dirty boy who buzzed around him like a persistent fly, positively asking to be swatted.

"Ah tell ya! T'monster's got 'em!"

"I already have your story. Now, lad—"

"Don't lissen t'him, lissen t'me!"

"That's enough now. Let someone else have a turn."

"But it's true! Ah saw 'em. They got horrid white eyes wi' holes in!"

"Shove off, or I'll lock you up. I've no time for jokes now."

"Ah tell ya! It's true! . . ."

One of the strangers said, "Is he the village

idiot? Why doesn't someone take him away?" Rob was bitterly offended.

It was the morning after the girls had disappeared, and it was still damp with dew. Yet already Boverley was crowded, with strange policemen, with volunteers from Charle and Ferne Bridge and Havershill. The vicar's wife took a weeping woman out of a car and led her into the vicarage; everyone was busy. They were going to search the moors.

"Hey, Rob, they've got six dogs," said one of his friends, jumping up and down with an excess of energy. "Alsatians! Smellers!"

"Smellers is bloodhounds," another boy said scornfully.

Rob ignored them. He had to make himself heard. Well, he *had* made himself heard. Now he had to get himself paid attention to—*respected*.

He caught hold of a passing policeman and said, "Ah've seen t'girls. Ah was with 'em when t'monsters—"

"See that nice policeman over there," said the man, pointing to the one Rob had just left. "You tell him all about it, lad. He'll be interested."

The search party was on the move—police, dogs, volunteers, and a lot of camp followers in the way of children and mothers trying to catch the children, before they, too, got lost on the moors.

"Come on, Rob," cried his friends, but he shook

his head sulkily. He knew where he wasn't wanted. Catching sight of the vicar, he made one last attempt.

"Tha angel's at t'bottom of our garden," he said.

"Not now, Rob, not now!" said the vicar, patting him on the head; then he hurried into the church.

The angel had let Rob down. Just when it could have been useful evidence that strange things could happen, that not all small boys were liars and that someone always had to see something for the very first time, so why not he, it had quietly turned back to stone. Last night, for some strange reason of its own, it had decided to chase after Rob. Perhaps because the choirboy reminded it of the churchyard that had for so long been its home. Perhaps it was tired of living and longed for the quiet of the graveside. All night it had stood in the hedge, looking up at Rob's window, waiting for him to come down and be caught.

When the sun rose it was still standing there, one finger now pointing to the sky, as if to say "Look! It's morning!" and a silly simper on its face, looking exactly as it had done all those years in the churchyard by Widow Carver's grave. Except that now it was standing in a hedge and covered with a fine web of cracks, as if the spiders had been busy. And on its ankle there was an odd mark, as if some dark metal had somehow fused into the stone.

Rob, getting up early, had first tried, unsuccessfully, to wake his snoring father, and then ventured into the garden. From a safe distance, he had thrown a brick at the angel. It had not moved. Coming nearer, he poked at it with a long stick. It had not moved. Old Prince, waddling past him, had sniffed the angel and then lifted his leg, mistaking it for a pillar. Even then it had not moved.

Rob had stared at it thoughtfully and kept his distance.

"Tha mustn't think Ah'm going t'trust ya," he'd said. "Ah'll never trust ya no more, tha great lumpen stone!"

And he had set off to find a policeman.

Now, disillusioned, he stood in the empty street, biting his fingernails, kicking pebbles, and brooding. Everyone had gone; up to the moors, having fun, back into their houses having breakfast, or into church to pray for the lost children. Even the young reporter from Havershill had ignored Rob. Stricken by a temporary blindness, he had hurried past the one boy who could have told him, for a modest sum, a tale to make his hair curl.

"And all *true!*" Rob muttered resentfully, decapitating one of the vicarage peonies that was unwise enough to show its head above the low garden wall. Guiltily looking up, he saw at the open window a grief-ravaged face, with swollen, red-rimmed eyes, a hand grasping the windowsill so tightly that the knuckles stood out like little ivory balls. One of the mothers, he decided.

He looked at her rather wistfully, thinking she must love her child a lot. He wondered whether to jump over the wall and try to tell her what he knew before anyone could stop him. But it was hardly comforting. Besides, would she believe him? Probably not. *Nobody* would believe him. One day they would be sorry. Rob wished that day would come before he was too old to care.

Mrs. Brown, standing at the vicarage window, twisted and turned the handkerchief in her hands as if she were trying to wring it dry.

The vicar's wife was making her some more tea. She had been very kind and not even hinted that it would have been better if Mrs. Brown had waited at home, like Emma's mother, since there was really nothing she could do here but stand and weep, and gaze up the empty road to the moors.

If she had stayed at Charle, Mrs. Brown could have kept herself busy, fiercely scrubbing floors, polishing tables, turning out cupboards, anything to fill the terrible gap before there was news. But after the long, long night's wait, she had felt she must get out, must look with her own aching eyes. Going up to Boverley had given her the illusion of joining in the search for Poppy, even though she knew she would be of no use on the moors. "You are not strong. You would only tire yourself out," they had said (and hold them up, but they had kindly not said that), "and we need you here."

So she had had to wait, standing by the window, twisting her wet handkerchief, and thinking . . . Thinking of all the times she had shouted at Poppy. Slapped her in a fit of temper. Dragged her over to the sink to scrub the back of her neck with a dish-cloth. Ordered her down on her knees to pray for God's forgiveness for her wicked lies.

It was I who was wicked, she thought now, though I never meant to be. I wanted to be a good mother, to bring her up to know right from wrong, to be a credit to me. But I was so tired! Always so tired and my bones aching! Each time I came out of the hospital, I'd ask for her back right away. Wait till you're stronger, they'd say, but I wanted her back there and then, my own daughter!

And there she'd stand, on the doormat, with her little suitcase and her paper bags full of kid's rubbish, and stare at me as if I were a stranger. Mother Brown, she calls me—like I was just one more foster mother. And not her favorite! How could I be? Worn out and irritable, old before my time, what was there for a child to love? I was never one who could show her feelings easy. Many a time I've wanted to say something nice, to give her a hug and a kiss, but she'd be off, joking with Mrs. Robbins, teasing Mr. Shepherd and playing with his dog. Free and easy with everyone except her own mother.

If Jack had lived, it would have been different. He knew how to be loving. He was a good husband and a good father, kissing came easy to him. After he died, it was like I turned to stone.

Up on the moors, the black Alsatian strained at his lead, pulling Constable Parks behind him as if he were trying to fly him like a kite. The dog was young and overeager and too easily forgot his training. Constable Parks loved him and tried to hide his faults, in case the dog would be taken away from him.

"Steady, boy," he said, and hoped nobody had noticed. The dog was sniffing and scrabbling now at the entrance to an old mine that was completely blocked by a rockfall. No child could possibly have gotten through. Even a rabbit would have had to be thin.

"Leave it!" he commanded, and pulled the dog on. "You're not supposed to chase rabbits. D'you want to be a *pet*?"

He was so anxious to shield his dog from possible blame that he did not notice something odd about the rockfall. Something, somehow, contrived. Nor did it occur to him that what can shut people out can also shut them in. Like his dog, he was young and inexperienced.

A helicopter flew backward and forward, backward and forward in the blue sky, and the sun shone. The search moved on.

It was evening before the searchers returned to Boverley, in ones and twos at first, and then a whole crowd of them. They were tired and dispirited, and shook their heads wearily when questioned, their own questions fading on their lips. Have they been found? Have you heard anything? Is there any news yet? No.

Emma's father and brother were the last back. They called at the vicarage to offer Mrs. Brown a lift back to Charle.

"You're not giving up? You *can't* give up!" she cried hysterically, pulling away from them, not wanting to get into the car. Wanting to go up on to the dark moors . . .

"The police now think they may not be on the moors at all," said Mr. Hodge. "They've a theory. . . . There was a robbery at Forster's last night. They think the girls might've witnessed it and been taken as hostages—"

"That's roobish, that is," said a grimy boy, gray as the twilight and seeming to appear from nowhere. "They's up on t'moors. Ah seen 'em last night. And that weren't no robbery neither, that were a walk-out! They's all up on t'moors, Ah tell ya! Won't nobody listen?"

"Go away, Rob," the vicar's wife said crossly.

Mr. Hodge opened the car door and began helping Mrs. Brown in. She looked once more up the empty road to the dark moors. . . .

"Look! Oh, look!" she cried, pointing. "What's that? There's a fire up there! Look, a fire!"

18

They heard the helicopter before they saw it. Then
suddenly there it was, very low, filling the whole
of their patch of sky. Before they had time to wave,
it had gone by, though they could still hear it,
buzzing backward and forward like a trapped
bluebottle.

They waited, but they did not see it again. The
sound of it grew fainter . . . louder . . . fainter . . .
louder again . . . as it circled the sky, and their
hopes swung with it. Then there was nothing left
but silence. It was gone.

Poppy swore.

"We're in the shadow," said Emma. "I don't
suppose they saw us."

They climbed down from their ledge, the rockfall making a rough staircase that even Emma
could manage, and sat hopefully in a patch of sunlight, ready to leap up shouting and waving. They
shared the last of the orange soda carefully be-

tween them and shook out the empty paper bag in search of crumbs. Gradually the sunlight moved. They followed it. It moved again.

"We'll be in the water soon," grumbled Poppy, helping Emma bump down the last rocks.

"Do you think it's fit to drink?" Emma asked doubtfully.

The sunlight did indeed gleam briefly on the dark water; then it was gone. The light was gray again and not very plentiful.

They won't come back now, thought Poppy. It'll be dark soon. Who knows if they'll find us tomorrow? Perhaps they'll call off the search altogether. Cross our names from the school register. Give our things to the Scout's jumble sale—my poor old teddy, my new dress, the silver bracelet Dad gave me when I was a baby. Mother Brown will find my diary on top of the wardrobe, read it, and be hurt. . . .

No! she thought. I'm getting out of here. I've been through so much—I'm not giving up now! If I have to claw my way out! She thought of the blocked-up entrance to the mine and glanced at her hands, so small and puny. She turned to look at Emma.

Emma was sitting, gnawing at the knuckle of her thumb for want of better sustenance and gazing at the dark tunnel. Seeing Poppy look at her, she said, "I'm not staying here, you know"—as if

Poppy had been trying to persuade her to. "I'm getting out of here if I have to swim for it."

Their separate trains of thought seemed to have arrived at the same station: the next stage of their journey was to be by canal.

It was ice cold in the water and black as night. Poppy went first, wading up to her waist and holding Emma's knapsack with their clothes and the precious box of matches in it well clear of the water. Emma swam behind. Now and then she bumped into Poppy or into one of the rock walls, but the very narrowness of the canal helped—there was no room to get lost.

It was a nightmare of a journey. Many times they were tempted to turn back, and only the thought that they might have come more than halfway made them go on. Then they worried in case they had passed the steps, missed them somehow—

"Are you sure th-they were on the left?" asked Emma, her teeth chattering.

"Yes," Poppy said firmly, and was immediately nagged by the thought, the conviction, that they had been on the right.

What was that? A very dark gray instead of black? Imagination? Wishful thinking? No! A shape . . . an edge . . . the edge of a step!

"I told you they were on the left!" She went splashing ahead and found herself at the bottom of the long flight of steps, dimly visible in the poor light. Light? She looked up and saw at the very top an irregular patch of sky.

Tears of relief came into her eyes.

"Emma! It's not blocked up anymore!" she cried joyfully.

She helped Emma out of the canal, scrambled into her clothes, and then, not bearing to wait while Emma hobbled slowly up the steps, ran on ahead, out of the mine and into the open air.

It was evening. A fine evening. A beautiful evening! Clouds blew across the wide, windy sky. A little way away, a courting couple sat on the grass, their arms around each other, their backs toward her. Never had she been so glad to see people before. She ran up to them, calling.

"Hullo! Can you help? My friend's hurt and we're lost!"

Why didn't they turn around? Were they deaf?

She went around to look at their faces, stopped, stared. . . . Terror seized her. How could she have mistaken them for real people? Why hadn't she guessed? How stupid she had been not to ask herself who had unblocked the entrance to the mine!

She backed away, her heart racing. Emma with her bad ankle! She must warn Emma!

"Why—why, it's Belladonna," she said very loudly, hoping her voice would carry, hoping Emma would have the sense to hide. She dare not look. "And lover boy! Waiting to catch us!"

As she spoke, her eyes looked over the darkening moors, choosing the way to run. Only she must make sure Emma was safe first.

The seated figures paid her no attention.

"Emma said we should *hide*," she went on, raising her voice on the last word. "Emma said we should *go the other way*. She'll be gone by now. Still, *I can run faster than you!*"

She was not very frightened, just cold. There was a wind blowing; running would warm her up. If only she could be sure Emma had gotten the message.

She began backing away again, watching the seated figures closely, taking no chances.

"Belladonna? Come and catch me?"

They did not move. Belladonna lay against the young shepherd's shoulder, her eyes closed as if in sleep, her lips faintly smiling, while he watched over her.

"You'll never catch me!" taunted Poppy, dancing about in front of them, trying to get them to chase her so that she could lead them away from Emma.

The statues were silent. They did not even glance at her. The wind blew a leaf against Belladonna's bare foot. It clung for a moment to her toes, fluttering. Her foot did not twitch. Her hand did not brush it away. *How long had they been there?* Had they forgotten the danger of the cracks?

"Belladonna?" Poppy said.

No response.

She stepped nearer. "Belladonna?"

How beautiful they were, the stone lovers. Even the fine web of cracks that covered them would not spoil their beauty. The shepherd boy smiled down at his sleeping girl as if he would never tire of looking at her.

"Which is just as well," Poppy muttered, "since that's the way it's going to be till the end of time. You can't move anymore, can you? But where did you learn about love? Not from me!" quite forgetting she had been prepared to lay down her life for her friend, and this is no little thing.

Perhaps they had never felt anything but merely, like rocks, echoed back the sounds of anger and war, and only when the battle was over had they been able to pick up the softer voice of love.

She touched the shepherd boy's cheek gently. It was cold and hard, the slight waxen feel gone. They had returned to stone. Proper stone. She looked at them as she shivered in the wind they could not feel. Or could they? Could they still feel the sun and the rain and the wind, only differently, in a stony sort of way?

Science was a mystery. She could never follow it at school. It was all a matter of atoms, of particles, dancing in different patterns. Perhaps we all had to make our own patterns. No good sticking feathers on and thinking we're birds, she thought ruefully. But at least we can learn to fly.

There was a slight noise behind her.

"You can come out, Emma!" she shouted. "It's safe! Look! They're dead of the cracks!"

Emma came limping out of the mine, shivering so much that she looked blurred, as if several Emmas had been parceled loosely together and were being shaken. Even so, thought Poppy, she looked better than any statue. A great warmth filled her for all the living, growing, imperfect world. Emma was human.

She could light a fire with only two matches, Emma said, given some dry grass and some wood. Only she couldn't be expected to fetch the wood, of course, not with her bad ankle.

"No, of course not," said Poppy, sighing, "I might've known! But where the blazes can I find wood up here?"

There were dead trees in that windbreak behind her, Emma pointed out. Meanwhile, Poppy needn't think she would be idle. The site needed careful preparation if they weren't going to set the whole moors alight. That great rock slab would do for a hearth. And if Poppy could just fetch her a few large stones? Mike says—

"I'll bet he does!" said Poppy, laughing.

Their fire took three matches but was otherwise a great success. It burned so brightly, it should have been visible for miles. Gradually Emma stopped shivering, and they lay back contentedly on the grass, waiting to be rescued.

"Food," Emma said dreamily. "Soup, sausages, potatoes..."

"I could eat a horse—" Poppy stopped abruptly and glanced at the sky.

"It's all right. You've already told a lie and nothing happened," said Emma.

"What? When?"

"When you were trying to warn me. You said I said it was better to hide. I didn't."

"I haven't been struck dead," said Poppy, pleased. She lay back and looked up to where the pink smoke and bright sparks rose up into the evening sky. The moon was already up and seemed to look down on her kindly. She had survived so much that she felt for the first time that perhaps God was kind.

"Silly, really," said Emma.

"What?"

"Thinking God would need your permission to strike you dead. Mike says people are always breaking promises to God and He must be sick of it all. Probably thought, cheeky brat, who does she think she is, choosing her own punishment? Let her live for a hundred years, that'll show her who's boss around here."

A hundred years?

"Done. I'll take it," said Poppy. She smiled up into the sky, feeling the firelight on her face, happy to be alive. What did it matter if her life wasn't exactly as she liked? Things couldn't be perfect. Be dull if they were. All those house mothers and foster mothers made for a lot of cards at Christmas. And her real mother? Oh, if she wasn't the plump, pretty, rich, kind mother she'd have chosen, that was just the luck of the draw. Poor old bonebag, thought Poppy, feeling a wave of affection for the stern, awkward woman who was her mother. Don't suppose she can help it. Things haven't been easy for her. Like me, for instance! Shouldn't have called her Mother Brown, knew she didn't like it. Mean, that was.

I'll never do it again, she decided. I'll call her Mother. I'll try to be friends. I'll change.

Which is more than they can do, she thought, catching sight of the stone lovers. The flickering light warmed them giving them an illusion of life, and she felt a moment's sadness. But perhaps they were happier in their strange, slow, imperceptible life, with the flowers at their feet, rising, blooming, and dying in a single stone moment, and the seasons spinning by, green and gold and white. Find your own pattern, Belladonna, she thought. Yours is a slower music than mine.

"They're our evidence," said Emma, following Poppy's glance. "People'd never believe us otherwise. Not with all the others buried under the rockfall. But they can't explain those away."

"They will," said Poppy. "They'll find some

sensible, practical, down-to-earth explanation, like it was dropped by helicopter. Or carried up here on the back of an elephant. Or a mad sculptor passing by had an irresistible urge to carve something. You'll see."

But she smiled, however, and putting her hand in her pocket, brought out a short length of greenish-black chain.

"Look what I found in the grass," she said.

"*Poppy!*"

"Just a small one?"

"*No!*"

"Not even a garden gnome?"

"NO!"

Poppy laughed and put the chain back in her pocket. Then she saw something that made her forget all about it. Lights bobbing up the hill. Figures approaching. Waving. Two of them started to run, shouting, "*Emma! Emma!*"

"Dad! Mike!"

Smiling, Poppy watched Emma hobbling off down the hill. Then she looked at the other people, not really expecting to see anyone she knew. There were policemen, men in ordinary clothes, and—a small figure jumping up and down, crying, "Ah told ya! Ah told ya!" Rob! More men . . .

Who was that right at the back? Struggling to keep up, stopping to fight for breath? A thin woman, with her hair blown all about and a white face. A woman who was not strong and who shouldn't have walked so far. . . .

"*Mom!*" cried Poppy, and went bounding joyfully over the grass.